Birth of the Firebringer

Meredith Ann Pierce

Birth of the Firebringer

FOUR WINDS PRESS
Macmillan Publishing Company ☆ New York
Collier Macmillan Publishers ☆ London

To Drew and Jill

Macmillan Publishing Company
866 Third Avenue, New York, N.Y. 10022
Collier Macmillan Canada, Inc.
Printed in the United States of America
10 9 8 7 6 5 4 3 2 1
The text of this book is set in 12 pt. Galliard.
Library of Congress Cataloging in Publication Data

Pierce, Meredith Ann.
Birth of the Firebringer.

Summary: Aljan, the headstrong son of the prince of the unicorns, becomes a warrior and discovers his destiny in his people's struggle against the hideous wyrms usurping their land.
[1. Unicorns—Fiction. 2. Fantasy] I. Title.
PZ7.P61453Bi 1985 [Fic] 85–42806
ISBN 0–02–774610–0

CONTENTS

BEGINNING

When Alma created the world, most of it she made into the Great Grass Plain, which was not a flat place, but rolling like a mare's back and covered all over with the greencorn and the haycorn and the wild oats, knee high, so that when the wind stirred it, billowing, it looked like a mare's winter coat blowing. And that is why some called the grasslands Alma's back. It was not the truth, for the Mother-of-all was not the world, but the Maker of the world.

With the stamp of one hoof, she made the Summer Sea, running shallow and warm even in wintertime. And with a little dig of her other heel, she raised the Gryphon Mountains upon its northern shore. Ranging north from there spread the dark Pan Woods, tangled and close, where only the blue-bodied goatlings roamed. Somewhere to the eastern north lay the Smoking Hills, where the red dragons denned, and due north across the Plain lay the Hallow Hills, a sacred place to the children-of-the-moon.

And that was all that was known of the world to the people I shall tell of in this tale. They lived in a great valley on the northern verges of the Woods. To the gryphons, they had always been a' ítichi, the enemy, and the pans murmured and gestured among themselves of the ufpútlak, four-footed walkers. The plainsdwellers, being near cousins to those of whom I speak, called them simply southlanders. But they named themselves the unicorns, which means the "one-horned ones," for each bore upon the brow a single spiral shaft as sharp as river ice and harder than hoof-breaking stone.

I am one of the fellows of this tale—I will not tell you which I am, though I promise that by the end of the running you will know me. My tale touches how the Firebringer came to be born among the unicorns, and what his coming meant to Aljan, son of Korr. But to start my tale, I must begin a little before the Firebringer, on a day near winter's end when Jan was six years old, nearly half-grown, though still counted among the colts. It had been a long, cold, dull winter, and the prince's son longed fiercely for the fiery storms of spring.

Stormclouds were rolling in out of the southeast. They darkened half the sky. It had been storming all day over the Gryphon Mountains, far on the horizon's edge. He had been watching the lightning there off and on since midmorning, flickering like great, violent fireflies, and he wondered whether the rain would spend itself before reaching the Vale of the Unicorns.

Jan paused on the trail heading upslope through the trees. He lifted his muzzle, his nostrils flared. The savor of moist earth and evergreens filled him. Winter was done, the snow gone from the ground, but it was not yet equinox. No new shoots sprouted on the slope, no new grass yet scattered among the stubble in the valley below. The year was just now struggling into birth, still in its storming month, the time of cold gales and showers before spring.

Jan lowered his head and shook himself, feeling his mane settle along his neck. He pawed the leaf mold with one cloven heel, swatted a pair of stinging gnats from his flank with his tassel-ended tail, and wondered where Dagg was. He and his friend had a standing agreement to meet on the hillside whenever a storm was in the wind. Jan nibbled at a fly bite on one shoulder, fidgeted. Then the sound of hoofbeats made him wheel.

Pale yellow and dappled with gray, Dagg was like most unicorn colts, the color of his sire. Jan was not—the prince's line never ran true, not since the days of Halla, four hundred summers gone. It was their mark, and set them off from all the herd, that no prince's heir might ever be a match for him, so while Korr was as black as the well of a weasel's eye, Jan, his son, was only sable, a rich dark brown like the color of earth. He spotted Dagg coming toward him through the trees.

Dagg neared and nipped at Jan, shouldering him, and the prince's son shied, kicking. They chased each other off the narrow trail, nickering and fencing with colts' long, unsharpened horns that clashed and clattered in the heavy, storm-awaiting stillness. Then Jan broke off, dodging back to the path, and sprinted toward the hillcrest.

"Hist, come on," he cried over one shoulder. "The storm's nearly here."

They sped upslope then through the patches of sunlight and shadows of the trees. Jan threw up his head, letting his long legs stretch. The wind fingered his mane and played through the shag of his winter coat. He felt young and strong and full of his own power. The rush of air laid back his ears. In another moment—in another moment, he would fly. Then he felt Dagg pulling up alongside him from behind and dropped back to a trot. They had nearly reached the top of the slope.

"Your father'll dance thunder if he finds out," Dagg said after a moment, "that we've come up this high, and with stormwind from the east."

Jan shook the forelock out of his eyes and nickered. Colts were forbidden to stray from the valley floor, away from the ready shelter of the grottoes there. The Gryphon Mountains rose barely a day's flight to the eastern south, and a gryphon could fly far with stormwind at its back. The unicorns lost foals every spring when the gryphon formels, the females, were hatching their ravenous young. Jan shrugged and laughed again. "We'll be back long before we're missed."

"Aye, and what if we meet someone up here?" Dagg asked him. "Then we'll catch a storm for sure."

"We won't," Jan told him. "With the rain so near, they'll all be under hill."

A great thorn thicket sprawled across their path. They began skirting it.

"But what about gryphons?" Dagg added uneasily. "They're bigger than unicorns." The yellow colt had dropped his voice. He crowded up against Jan's flank.

Jan shook him off. "Wingcats only hunt the east side of the Vale. We're in the west. And my father the prince lives here—they'd never dare."

Dagg looked dubious.

Jan snorted and sprang away. "Know what I'd do if I ever saw a gryphon?" The prince's son reared, pawing the air. "I'd give it such a blow, it'd never rise again! I'd . . ."

Then all at once he caught sight of something: motion, a shape. Choking off his words, he dropped to all fours and gazed ahead through the thick of the trees. The hillcrest lay not far upslope. They had nearly rounded the thorns. When Dagg started to speak, Jan shushed him with a hiss.

"What is it?" breathed Dagg.

Jan shook his head. He edged forward, peering. All he could discern through the undergrowth was a vague form, some animal. It was large and stood in shadow among the trees. A cold sensation touched Jan's breast. Neither he nor any colt he knew had ever seen a gryphon, but the singers spoke of great hawk beaks and wings, talons, cat's eyes, and hind limbs like those of the saber-toothed pards that roamed the Plain.

Dagg pressed against him, making him jump. "Can you make it out?"

Jan shook his head again and crept closer, putting his hooves down soundlessly. With so many trees blocking his view, he still could not determine any outline he recognized, and strained instead for a glimpse of vivid green and gold—the colors of a tercel, a gryphon male—or of blue and tawny—a formel.

The creature on the hillside shifted its stance. Jan froze and felt Dagg beside him flinch. Jan felt the stinging gnats at his flank again and did not swat. They waited long seconds. He edged his eye slowly around a treebole and caught a clear view of the hillcrest at last through a gap in the trees.

It was . . . another unicorn. Only that. Another unicorn. Jan snapped his teeth together and could have kicked. Of course it would be one of his own people. Of course! He had forgotten the lookouts. This crest commanded a view of the east. The prince must have ordered watches to scan the stormwind, because it was spring now. Gryphons never came in winter. He should have remembered that. Jan stood absolutely still.

Dagg nudged him urgently. "What's there?" he whispered. "Can you see it now?"

"One of ours," Jan muttered. "My father's . . . oh, it's Tek."

He stopped again, recognizing the other suddenly, for the lookout had stepped from the shadows into the sun. She was not the solid or dapple or roan of other unicorns, but paint: pale rose splashed with great, irregular blots of black.

"What, the healer's daughter?" Dagg was asking, his voice beginning to rise as though he no longer cared whether they were discovered or not. "We're done for storming then."

"Hist," Jan told him, eyeing the lookout still.

She was a strange one, so he had heard. He hardly knew her. A fine warrior, all agreed, but very aloof and always alone—just like her mother, Jah-lila, who was the healer's mate but did not live among the herd. The wild mare who lived apart, outside the Vale. Jah-lila the midwife, the magicker.

Jan eyed the young paint warrior Tek through the trees; and as he did so, a part of his mind that he usually kept tightly guarded, opened—and a plan came to him, insinuating itself into his thought like swift, smooth coils. Jan felt his pulse quicken and his dark eyes spark.

"Hist," he said again to Dagg. "Let's test this lookout's skill." He shouldered the other back into the shadow of the trees. "I have a game."

Jan kept his voice beneath a murmur and whispered the whole of his plan in two sentences. Then he and Dagg parted, and Jan lost sight of the dapple colt among the firs. Quickly, quietly, he himself circled back to the lookout knoll. Peering from behind a bit of ledge and scrub, he caught sight of Tek again. She stood facing away from him, her head turning slowly as she scanned the wall of cloud rolling in from the southeast. Jan waited.

And presently he heard a noise downslope. Tek's ears swiveled, pricked, but she did not turn. Jan watched intently, but as the sound died Tek's ears turned forward again. She scanned the sky. Jan breathed lightly, one breath, two; he held his breath. Then the noise came again, closer, clearer this time. Tek's ears snapped around. Jan champed his teeth. But again the sound ceased and quiet followed. The prince's son settled himself to wait.

The sound came for a third time, suddenly, much nearer, a low, throaty mewling such as the storytellers said gryphon hatchlings made. Jan found himself tense and shivering; his skin twitched. How real it sounded—Dagg was the best mimic of all the uninitiated foals. Tek's head now had whipped around, her frame gone rigid. A rustling started in the thorn thicket. Jan had to duck his chin to keep from nickering. The half-grown mare on the lookout knoll stood head up, legs stiff.

Silence. Jan saw Tek's green eyes searching the brush. She touched the ground, pawing it gently, her eyes narrowed and her nostrils flared. Jan heard more gryphon cries downslope—just exactly as they sounded in the lays. Tek's forehoof dug into the earth. He edged closer, keeping himself concealed. The young warrior's movements fascinated him.

He heard Dagg rustling in the thickets again, and saw Tek bowing her head to polish the tip of her skewer-sharp horn deftly against one forehoof. He had seen half-growns as well as the full-grown warriors doing that before battle. Then suddenly a sharp yell, like that of a wounded wingcat, rang out, and the sound of bushes crashing. Jan could almost believe it was a real gryphon blundering downslope. Tek sprang away, into the trees, so swift Jan almost lost her in a blink, for she ran silent, and gave no warning cry.

Jan shook himself. He felt elated—it had worked! Satisfaction slithered through him as he emerged from the trees and mounted the lookout knoll. He heard Dagg circling the crest of the ridge, giving cries now like an injured tercel, now like an angry formel. No sound came from Tek, and the prince's son wondered if his friend was even aware yet of her pursuit. He hoped so. He needed the lookout kept away long enough for him to watch the storm.

Jan stood on the crest of the knoll. The clouds before him were sweeping in fast. He felt the cool, muggy air beginning to lift, a faint breeze teasing along his back. It grew stronger suddenly, blew, smelling of rain. The thunderheads rolled, black foaming waves that scudded toward the sun. Unseen lightning illumined them in glimmers, like mosslight glimpsed beyond cavern bends.

Thunder sounded in a low growling that crashed all at once like a hillside falling. Jan felt the concussions against his body, and threw back his head to let the thick, cold, wet wind buffet him. He watched the shadow of the storm travel over the Pan Woods below him till a bank of cloud extinguished the sun. The world went gray. Birdfoot lightning gripped the sky.

The clouds loomed high, almost above him, over the Vale. As he gazed up into their wild, dark roiling, it seemed to Jan he could see—almost see—*something*. The sweep of them was like stars turning, like billowing grass, like mighty flocks of birds wheeling, like unicorns dancing, like . . . *like* . . . . He could not say what it was like. He only knew that when he gazed at the storm and lost himself, feeling the whirling turbulence of its power, his heart rose, carried away, soaring, and all the world rode on his brow.

Below him, a few lengths down the slope, Jan heard a whinny from Dagg suddenly and knew that his friend was caught. Above the muting of the wind, Jan heard Dagg's shouts of laughter, his protestations, and now Tek's voice, stinging with anger. Jan snorted and shook his head, only half listening. A dark exhilaration still fired his blood as he watched the dance of stormclouds swallow up the sky.

A pair of hunting eagles, huge ones, dipped out of the clouds far in the distance over the Pan Woods. They were in his sight for only a moment, stooping swiftly into the cover of the trees. He caught only the poise of their wings crooked for the dive and their size, great enough to carry off a young pan between them.

Just before they reached the trees, a blaze of lightning flashed. The deep green of the foliage reflected off their tawny bodies for an instant, turning the near one greenish, the far one almost blue. They plunged into the forest then. Jan lost them amid the canopy of trees.

Almost at the same moment, the sound of breaking brush distracted him. He turned in time to see Tek shoving Dagg out of the trees into the clearing of the knoll. Dagg was laughing so hard he staggered. The half-grown mare clamped the nape of his neck in her teeth and hauled him back as he made half heartedly to bolt. She stood taller than either he or Jan, and had been initiated a full two years ago. Her young beard was already silky on her chin.

"Gryphons—save me!" shouted Dagg, struggling some, but laughing harder. "I told you it wasn't my game. Ouch! Not so hard—it was Jan's. The whole of it was Jan's."

"I know that very well, Dagg son-of-Tas," replied his captor through clenched teeth. She released him, and Dagg collapsed to the carpet of fir needles at the wood's edge. He rolled there, hooting. "I have heard of the games you two are so fond of." She turned now toward Jan. "And you, prince-son. By Korr, *you* at least should know better."

Jan tossed his head, laughing in his teeth, and shrugged. His father—no, he would not think of Korr. The prince was far below, seeking shelter in the Vale from the coming rain, and Jan was free of him for a little while at least. Free. He sprang down from the lookout knoll and trotted to Dagg, eyeing the hairless patches on his friend's neck and flank.

"Are you hurt?"

Dagg groaned, laughing still. "Hale enough. She champs *hard*. By the Beard, Jan, you should have seen her when she realized I wasn't some storm-riding gryphon."

Dagg rolled his eyes, ears akimbo, nostrils flared, and tossed his head like one who had just trod upon a snake. Jan put his head down, helpless with mirth. He laughed until his legs felt weak.

"Both of you have borne yourselves like brainless foals," the young mare snapped. "You, Jan son-of-Korr, haven't you grace enough to speak when you're spoken to?" Jan ignored her. Her tone crackled. "I am talking to you."

She marked that, when the prince's son neither answered nor turned, by nipping him smartly on the shoulder. Jan jumped and wheeled. Disbelief, and a sudden odd heedlessness uncoiled in him. No one had ever set teeth to him, not in earnest, but his father. No one had ever dared. He felt the blood surging in his head. His ears grew hot.

"You champed me!" he cried.

Dagg on the ground had swallowed his grin.

"You set teeth to me."

"Aye, and I'll do so again the next time you ignore me. What have you to say for yourself?"

Jan stared at her. Not even a word of regret—the arrogance! The astonishment in him turned to rage. He'd let no one, not even the healer's daughter, treat him like a foal. He plunged at her, his head down, before he was even aware what he was doing—perhaps a slash across the flank would teach this half-grown better manners. Tek countered with her own horn, fencing him expertly, and threw him off with a sharp rap on the head.

Jan staggered, startled. He had always been the victor, the easy best in the mock battles among the uninitiated colts. Now—first bitten, then baited, then parried in three blows. Jan regained his footing and stood stunned, humiliated. A cold little voice in the back of his mind teased and taunted him, but he shoved it away, shoved everything away. His breath was coming hard between clenched teeth. Tek had not fallen back even a step.

Dimly, he came aware that Dagg beside him was speaking. "Jan. Hear me. She's half-grown." His friend started to rise. "Colts don't spar with warriors. List, come on, let's . . . ."

Jan ignored him, flattening his ears. He was not a colt, not just *any colt.* He was the son of the prince of the unicorns, and he would not be beaten off a second time. Tek snorted, shifting her stance. She squared to meet him. He lowered his head, gathering his legs.

"Enough!"

The word rolled hard and deep above the rising wind. Jan pulled up, startled, spinning around. Tek glanced past him, and he glimpsed her falling back now in surprise. The prince of the unicorns stood before them on the lookout knoll, black against the grayness of the storm. Lightning clashed, throwing a blue sheen across him. Jan flinched at the suddenness, feeling his rash temper abruptly vanish, like a snake into a hole. He gazed uneasily into his father's dark and angry eyes.

"Leave off these foals' games," ordered the prince. "You, Dagg, son of my shoulder-friend, off home with you—at once."

Jan felt his friend beside him scrambling to his feet. Dagg bowed hastily to the prince, then wheeled and was gone. His hoofbeats on the slope grew faint.

"You, Tek, healer's daughter, begone as well."

"Prince," Tek started, but he shook his head.

"Rest sure, young mare, I put no blame on you in this."

"Korr, prince," she said, "I am on lookout. . . ."

He tossed his head then. "Never mind. No gryphons will be flying once the rain comes. Now off, or you will be soaked."

Tek bowed her long neck to the prince, then wheeled and bounded away like a lithe deer through the trees. Korr waited until the gusting wind had swept the sound of her heels away.

"Foal!" he burst out then, and Jan flinched beneath his father's rebuff. "Witless thing! Have I not expressly forbidden any colts so high on the slopes, and warned all against interfering with the lookouts?"

Jan eyed his hooves and mumbled assent.

"Can you not understand gryphons may slip into these woods under cover of cloud in two bats of an eye? A moment's distraction . . ." He broke off with a strangled snort.

Jan hung his head. His father spoke the truth; he remembered the hunting eagles, how swiftly they had fallen from cloudbottom to treetops while Dagg had been baiting Tek. What if, rather than hawks, there had come wingcats instead? Jan picked at the turf with his hoof.

"It was just a game," he murmured, more to

himself than to Korr. "We meant no harm."

"Your *games,*" muttered Korr. "But enough."

The black prince launched down from the lookout knoll and gave his son a shove to turn him. "Be grateful this storm's brought no gryphons, young princeling, or you might well have made feast-flesh for some formel's hatchlings—or Tek might, or Dagg. Hie now! Get you home."

Jan sprang down the slope, his pace abruptly quickened by a few hard nips on the flank from his father. He galloped blindly, careless of the hillside's steepness, reckless where he set his hooves. The prince ran beside him, herding him away from the sheer drops, the loose rock shelves.

Jan ducked, dodging through the trees. He wished he could fly, fly away and outpace his father. His breast was tight, his eyes stinging. All he had wanted to do was watch the storm. Nothing, no ill would have come of it if it had not been for Tek. Arrogant half-grown! Jan wished the pied mare bad footing.

How he hated the young warriors, half-grown, already initiated—hated, yet in the same breath envied them. He was weary to death of colts' games and foals' playing, and longed to the center of his bones to be allowed to sharpen his hooves and horn and join the Ring of Warriors. *Why* had

Korr held him back from Pilgrimage last year, despite his pleading?

Deep down, he knew. And thinking of it brought a bitter taste into his mouth. There was in his nature a grievous fault. He could never do as he was told, as others did. He always plunged ahead without thinking, forgetting the Law—or deliberately breaking it. He was a vexation to everyone, a bitter disappointment to Korr, and secretly he wondered if he would ever learn to bear himself as befitted the prince's son.

Jan plunged down the steep hillside. A stitch had grown between his ribs. It ached like a wound. He and his father left the wooded slope for the rolling meadow of the valley floor. The sky above was wholly dark. Jan felt a great drop splash against his back, soaking into the long hairs of his winter coat. Another drop struck him, and then two more. The air was thick suddenly with falling water. He heard Korr snorting in disgust.

They headed across the open meadow toward their cave halfway up the near slope of the Vale. Korr sprang onto the rock ledge before the cave mouth, Jan scrambling up behind. The entrance to the grotto was narrow. In the gloom beyond, Jan saw his mother, Ses, cream colored with a mane as amber as autumn grass. She was heavy in foal.

Korr moved two steps into the cave, tossing his head, and the water slung from his long, jet mane. Jan crowded in behind, out of the rain, though he knew by his father's abrupt, forceful movements that he was angry still. The prince of the unicorns shook himself, and Jan ducked, but he could not avoid the spray short of retreating into the rain again. His mother stood back out of range.

"A wet day for bathing," she laughed when Korr was done. "How clement of the weather to soak you both so handsomely." Her light, sure tone seemed to mollify her mate a little. "Jan, come out of the door now; you're wet enough. Korr, let him by."

Jan saw his father glance over one shoulder at him. The prince advanced a pace, no more, cleaning the muck from between the toes of his hooves with his horn. "I found him up on the high slopes again," he said shortly, "near the lookout knoll."

Jan saw his mother's eye grow rueful for a moment, but then she smiled. "But he always goes up there. You know that. He always has."

"It's forbidden," his father snapped. "And not just to Jan—to all the colts. It's too dangerous, especially when the storm's from the southeast." Korr gave a snort. "He had Dagg with him. Bringing others into his Ringbreaking."

His father started on another hoof. Jan had to shrink past him along the wall. He saw his mother glance at him, then felt a few strokes of her rough, dry tongue against his neck, pressing out the damp. He hadn't dared to shake off yet, and now his mother's gentle tolerance was suddenly more than he could bear. He broke from her, from Korr, and clattered away from both of them, deeper into the cave.

Around the bend at the back of the hollow, a little pool of earthwater lay, still as stone, reflecting the dim light rounding the corner. Pale toadstools and lichens scattered the walls and shore, casting faint illuminations. Jan threw himself down on the pebbly bank and lay there wet and miserable. Staring at nothing, he listened to the voices of his sire and dam.

"If that were all," his father's deep voice said, "if that were all, I might let it pass. But Ses, the colt has no sense. He and Dagg weren't on the ridge just to watch the storm."

Jan heard a sigh. "More games?"

Silence a moment. Korr must have nodded. "They were baiting the lookout, drawing her away with gryphon cries. What am I to do with him? That's willful trespass. . . ."

"Be patient with him," the prince's mate was saying. Then, softer, "He was born under a dark moon."

Jan dropped his head to the bank and felt his heart clench shut like teeth. He wished she wouldn't defend him—he wished there weren't the need. There was the sound of someone shifting. Jan imagined his mother lying down beside her mate, helping to sponge the rest of the moisture from his coat.

"He's moody, high-spirited."

"Unruly," the prince returned. "A hothead."

"Like you."

"Love, he's not a colt anymore!" Jan flinched at the force of his father's anger.

"He is until you let him join the initiates." His mother's sudden vehemence surprised him. "How often has he begged you to let him go on Pilgrimage?"

Jan heard his father's snort. "How can I, now? Do you think he'd make a warrior? He's nearly half-grown, and still he acts like a spoiled weanling. That wildness . . ." Jan hardly caught the last. What had his father said: "*frightens me*"? No, he could not have heard it right.

"Just let him prove himself," his mother murmured. "More than anything, he wants to prove himself."

Their voices grew softer, dropping into quiet unintelligibility beneath the drumming of the rain. Jan stretched his forelegs in front of him, laying his head along their length. Born under a dark moon. *Dark moon,* she'd said. He stared off into the darkness, with its wan lichenlight, brooding.

He must have dozed, for the next thing he knew was that the grotto had grown a little lighter, and the sound of the rain had stopped. He lifted his head from his knees, blinking and feeling stiff from sleep. He had dreamed something—he was aware of that, but could not remember what. He never remembered his dreams. Jan plucked a pale toadstool from the shore and ground its musty, woody flesh across his teeth, trying to remember. From the light reaching him around the bend, he guessed it must be midafternoon.

The dream had been something about the water, or something in the water. Something swimming in the lichenlight, like a longfish, or an eel. Had it stood up before him, the white thing in the water? Swaying and flickering like . . . like . . . he could not say what. The image faded from him even as he strained for it. But he remembered he had shuddered, squirming as he looked at it, unable to turn away. And it had spoken his truename: Aljan, *dark moon*.

When he had been very young, scarcely weaned, he had begun to have such dreams: dreams of snakes and stinging worms that woke him struggling, screaming night after night, till others of the herd began to mutter that the prince's son must be accursed. Korr, in desperation, had sent for the healer's mate, Tek's mother, Jah-lila, to come and steal away Jan's dreams.

He had been so little then, it had been so long ago, and he had not seen the wild mare since. She rarely ever came into the Vale, and then always secretly, silently, like a shadow barely glimpsed; and she was gone again in an hour, about whatever business a magicker's business might be, of which she never spoke. He remembered only dimly that time she had come to him, while his parents had stood back silent, troubled, out of the way. Dark rose in color, Jah-lila had knelt, lying down beside him, gazing into and through him with her black-green eyes.

"Ho, little hotblood," she had murmured. "Such a fighter, such a dreamer! Eat this now, and breathe in this. Sleep . . . *dreamless* . . . sleep."

She had given him bitter herbs to eat and chewed sweet herbs herself, breathed upon him and let him breathe her breath. He had slept then, at once, deep and restfully. And since that time he had never been able to remember his dreams.

Jan finished the last of the woody toadstool and sipped from the dark cave pool beside him. The water was cool, tasteless. He watched the ripples widen and still. When the surface grew eye-smooth again, the lichens reflected there like a scatter of rose and pale blue stars. From the outer chamber, he heard his mother murmuring, as she had used to do for him, a lullaby to her unborn foal:

> *"Hist, my lambling, quiet now,*
> *Lest a waiting wingcat hear*
> *With ears up-pricked and eyes aglow—*
> *Hush! Let him not find you, little pan.*
> *Still your cry, lie soft, and sleep."*

Jan felt himself just slipping into sleep again. He clicked his teeth, stifling a yawn, when all at once something caught his eye. He blinked. The surface of the cave pool beside him was dancing. The images of the lichens trembled there. Sounds like something scraping, then sliding reached his ears. The pebbles beneath him shifted and seethed. There came a sudden rumbling roar in which the whole cave shuddered. Chips of stone from the ceiling fell. Dust rose in the air like winter fog.

He heard his mother whinnying, his father snorting, choking on dust. Jan scrambled to his legs and dashed into the forepart of the grotto. A great rock shard from overhead smashed to the floor barely a pace from him. He shied and, as he did so, glimpsed Ses dodging out the cave's entrance into the light.

He sprang to follow, then stopped himself in a sudden panic. Where was Korr? Jan wheeled, casting about him through the dimness, through the dark, crying his father's name. Then he heard the prince's deep voice, "Go on!" and felt Korr's massive frame shouldering him through the cave mouth into the outside air.

Jan plunged through a rain of earth. Stones, some large as skulls, crashed with the rest. The rock ledge ahead was nearly buried. He saw his mother moving heavily down the muddy, sliding slope to solid ground on the valley floor below.

Jan felt a great concussion and wheeled to see Korr shying from a boulder's path. It smashed to fragments. Jan felt a splinter dig into the flesh of his thigh. He stumbled, the soft earth sliding beneath his hooves. Muddy soil and pebbles pelted him as he struggled to rise—then his father's teeth closed over the nape of his neck, half dragging, half hauling him out of the muck.

Jan's legs gave beneath him as he reached the valley floor. The pain in his injured leg was fierce.

Ses was standing well back, out of the path of the slide, and he was aware, dimly, of other unicorns dashing from their caves, crying out in consternation, galloping toward them over meadow and slope. Jan tore his gaze back to the grotto.

He saw the last of the rain-softened earth cascading down the slope, the broken stone and fragments of the great, smashed boulder . . . and then, above that, a flash of green, dusty blue, and gold. Two gryphons, a mated pair, perched on an outcropping above the cave. With an uprooted sapling, they levered root and soil, sending it surging down the hillside.

Gryphons. Jan felt cold talons seize his heart. He remembered the flash of color, the two wingèd forms he had glimpsd from the lookout. Not eagles, *gryphons*—who had slipped into the Pan Woods beneath his very gaze.

Jan heard his father trumpeting a war cry. Then a second cry sounded, joining Korr's. Turning, Jan saw Dagg's father, Tas. Other battle yells rose on the air: stallions trumpeting full and deep and wild, high clarions from the mares. Jan saw the wingcats dropping their lever, beginning to scramble up the hillside as Korr and a half-dozen others charged the slope.

Jan staggered to his feet, moving to join them, but Ses swung in front of him, barring his path. "No, Jan," she told him. "Let the warriors have it."

He tried to dodge her, but his bad leg made

him slow. She caught him by the nape of the neck.

"Let go," he cried. "They made to trap us. They wanted to kill Korr!"

He struggled furiously. His mother's strong, square teeth only clasped tighter. "No," she panted. "You're not a warrior."

"But I will be," Jan shouted, fighting harder. "This spring I'll be initiated. . . ."

"Not *yet,*" Ses answered. His bad leg gave as she forced him to the ground and stood over him. Jan clenched his teeth, his ears burning with wrath. There was nothing he could do.

He watched the hillside. The two gryphons had reached the crest of the unwooded slope. Now they reared upon their hind limbs, beating their wings, but the draggled pinions seemed unable to get a purchase on the air. Jan felt his blood quicken as he realized the warriors would catch them.

The larger gryphon, the formel, launched into the air and hovered unsteadily, her blue wings laboring. Her mate's wings, still streaked with mud, seemed as yet too heavy to fly. With a shout, the prince of the unicorns charged and drove his horn into the tercel's side.

Cat snarl rising to a falcon's scream, the wingcat lashed back. Jan heard his mother's little snort of breath as the prince of the unicorns went down—but then he rolled and was up again in a moment, hammering the gryphon with his hooves.

The unicorn warriors ringed the tercel. Tas seized one talon; others stabbed at his great, green wings. The gryphon fought, raged, broke free of their circle at last and retreated, one pinion dragging. The formel stooped and feinted in the air above.

Jan saw the wounded tercel rise, his wingbeats ragged. He hovered, struggling, above the warriors' heads. Jan saw his father backing, his hindquarters bunched. Korr leapt, catching the wingcat in the belly. The tercel shrieked, wrenching away. The formel clutched him in her claws.

The unicorns watched their uneven flight, the gryphons staggering through the air toward the south. They trailed low over the ridges ringing the Vale. The tercel's wingbeats slowed suddenly, grew more erratic. The formel labored to bear him up. They barely cleared the lookout knoll.

Then the wounded wingcat stiffened. His green-gold pinions thrashed, stretched taut. His body sagged in the formel's grasp and a long, hoarse scream rose from his mate; her wings beat strong and frantically. Jan could not discern whether she would not release him even then, or whether his talons still clutched her so tightly she could not pull free. Together they plunged into the trees beyond the ridge.

The unicorns were coming down the slope. Korr leaned against Tas, blood running down the prince's neck. He bled from a gash above one eye. Jan realized Ses no longer stood above him. He rose with difficulty and stood, three-legged, putting no weight on his injured leg.

"Where's the healer?" Jan heard Tas calling, as he and the prince reached the bottom of the hill.

Ses went to Korr. Other unicorns were moving forward. They drifted around him. Jan alone stood still.

"No, it's a scratch," his father was saying, but the prince's voice was breathless, all thunder gone. Someone brushed past him, and Jan caught a glimpse of Teki, the healer, moving toward Korr. Fear, like a sea-jell, lay cold on Jan's breast.

He felt someone else slip up beside him. "Are you hale, Jan? Your leg's bleeding."

Jan shook his head, blinking hard, and did not turn.

Dagg seemed to take no notice. "By the Circle, I never thought I'd see a real one, a gryphon! I never thought they'd dare come here. And after the prince . . . !"

Jan drew in his breath and held it then, for he felt somehow he might begin to shake, or fall, if he so much as breathed. Ses and Tas were supporting Korr back upslope a little way, toward better light. Teki followed them, his distinctive white and black coloring catching the sun. The valley floor was slipping into shade.

" . . . you go with them?" he heard Dagg saying. "The healer should look at you, too."

And suddenly Jan did not think he could bear to be near another living creature, even Dagg. He wheeled, bolting away from his friend, and struck out across the meadow toward the near wooded slope. He had no earthly notion of where he was going, but he had to be alone.

Jan sprinted toward the wooded slopes, his thoughts in a roil. He felt the others were looking at him, as though his guilt somehow blazed visible. But more than that, he feared Korr knew. It was *his* fault gryphons had slipped into the Vale, his fault his father had been wounded.

How badly? Jan shoved the thought away and galloped harder as the floor of the valley turned upward. The splinter of stone in his thigh muscle gouged him, but the shame he felt stung him more. He was unworthy—he had always known. Unworthy of Korr or to be called the prince's heir. *Why* was he so different from others? He clenched his teeth against the tightness in his throat, and fled into the trees.

It was late afternoon. The clouds above had spent themselves and were pulling apart like wet seed tufts. Swatches of the yellow sky shone through. Jan climbed a little way, then rested, surveying the wood about him bleakly. Droplets glistened on the fir needles; the cedar bark was damp. The sun hung westering, and everything smelled clean.

His injured leg had begun to ache in earnest now. The thigh muscle felt strained. Jan nibbled at the wound, working the splinter free, then spat it out, tasting blood: It had cut his tongue. He climbed on. When he reached the lookout knoll, he found Tek standing there and halted, startled. She wheeled.

"You," she cried, her eyes bright, throat tense. "And what brings you back, prince's son—come to gaze on the sunset after the storm?"

Jan stood, hardly knowing what to say. "I came to be alone," he managed.

She studied him. "I saw what befell," she said. Her voice was husky. "From across the meadow—the gryphons. I'd just emerged; the others were all still under hill. I saw a form of green and gold, then one of tawny blue come down the far hillside, dragging a great tree limb. They began to lever up the rock and earth above your grotto. I gave a cry—I don't think anyone heard—but I was too far away to join the warriors."

Jan gazed at her, but could think of nothing. "My father's wounded."

Tek nodded. "My father was sent for."

Jan eyed his hooves. The breath caught in his throat. "It's my doing," he mumbled.

Tek threw up her head, eyes flashing. He thought at first it was with anger. "You?" she cried, and he realized then it was with astonishment. "*I* was the one posted lookout." Her voice grew tighter, almost choking. She gasped between clenched teeth. "But I let myself be tricked away . . . oh! Just like a foal not yet a warrior. Just like an uninitiated foal."

Jan started to interrupt. "No. I saw them from afar. I thought . . ." But then he choked himself off, realizing what she had said. *Initiation.* The spring rite of Pilgrimage lay less than a month off.

Each new year, as soon as the forage had sprung upon the Great Grass Plain, the prince of the unicorns led a chosen band to the sacred well of their race. A few of the band were warriors, acting as escorts; the rest, initiates, those fillies and foals adjudged worthy of drinking from the well. In doing so, they would cast off their childhood and join the Ring of Warriors.

Jan and Dagg had hoped to join the Circle this season, together, though Dagg was younger than the prince's son. Jan's parents had held him back from Pilgrimage the spring before—it was not uncommon. His mother had said gently that he needed another year of colt's play. Korr had told him more curtly that his hot head needed to cool.

Jan felt a sinking in his chest. Korr would hold him back again—the thought stung him more sharply than shame. He would be scorned, thought of forever not as the prince's son, but as the young firebrand who had let the gryphons in and was not fit to be made a warrior. And he knew what became of those who never drank of the well in the sacred rite of passage. He had heard the fate of Renegades in singers' tales.

They ceased to be unicorns. Banned from the herd, they saw their horns rot to the skullbone and fall away, their heels lose their fringe of feathery hair and their ears their tufted tassels. No fine, soft beards ever sprouted along their chins. Their cloven hooves grew together, each into a single toe: strange solid hooves that left round imprints in the dust. Renegades grew old before their time, and died young.

Jan started suddenly, coming back to himself. He saw Tek's green eyes on him from the lookout knoll.

"He'll hold me back," he blurted out. "My father will keep me from the rite again."

Tek's gaze had lost its hardness. She nodded a bare trace and said quietly, "Aye, princeling. I think he may."

Anguish welled in Jan. What could he do? Despair enveloped him and he felt himself sliding down its dark throat toward nothing. The prince would make no announcement. Nothing would be said at large—he would not be publicly disgraced.

But everyone would hear of it. His unworthiness would be revealed at last. It would be known—it would be known! Panic gripped him. Jan wheeled, clenching his teeth to keep from crying out, and bolted away into the trees. Tek called after him, but did not follow. Her shouts soon faded.

He found himself running along the ridge and plunged over the hillcrest down the wooded slope. He was on the far side now, the side that faced the Pan Woods. This was forbidden territory, even to warriors—but no matter. Better to wander the rest of his days in the goatling woods than to go back disgraced and face another year denied the Ring.

He halted suddenly and bowed his head, running the tip of his horn along the outer edge of each forehoof once, twice, a half dozen times in short, unpracticed strokes. This, too, was forbidden. Colts were banned from sharpening their hooves and horns. By Law, only the warriors were allowed.

But he was an outcast now, a Renegade, and must be his own Law. And if the pans came upon him in the woods, he meant to draw their blood before they dragged him down. He ran on then, blindly, fleeing a great, looming fear he could not name. He wished the earth might open and swallow him.

Without warning the ground beneath him shifted, gave way suddenly, and he was plunging. Rain-soaked soil crumbled about his legs and he slid headlong, dropping abruptly, and landed with a jolt that knocked the breath from him. Something tumbled past his head, struck him a glancing blow behind the ear, then thudded softly to the dirt beside him. A stone.

The place was very dim; he could scarcely see.

Straining for breath, he shook his head. It was exceedingly quiet. The fall of earth and rock had made almost no sound. He lay a few moments, his legs folded awkwardly beneath him, a little stunned, and not at all certain what had just happened.

His head cleared. His breath came back, and Jan was able to take in his surroundings. He lay on a heap of earth in the narrow opening of a cave, a mere crack in the hillside, very close and dark. Glancing up, he saw some of the roof overhanging the grotto's mouth must have collapsed when he stumbled across it. And a good thing, too, he realized with a start, or else in his blind gallop he might have run right off the cliff.

He picked himself up warily, still giddy with relief. None of his bones seemed to be broken. Only his bad leg hurt. He stood now half in, half out of the cave, and the sky behind him was brightening to flame. What rags of cloud were left were infused with red. A little of that light reflected off the lip of the entryway.

Jan peered ahead of him into the dimness, but could make out nothing. He listened, hearing nothing. The narrow space smelled old and goaty. But presently, his nostrils quivered as a new scent reached him, strange and musky—not one he recognized. Jan frowned, breathing deeper, and limped forward a few paces into the earthy darkness of the cave.

His eyes had grown accustomed now, and he discerned the uneven wall opposite the one near which he stood, the continuation of the grotto's crevice back into the rock. He started forward again—but halted suddenly. A large mound lay at the back of the cave, just before where the chamber narrowed to a crack too close and dark to see beyond.

The half-light from the outside had grown warmer, redder as the unseen sun dropped lower in the sky. Jan's vision improved: tawny fur and azure feathers. The musky odor swam in his head. At the back of the grotto, not five paces from him, lay some animal. . . .

His heart contracted, jerking him back. Jan recognized a gryphon curled upon its side, wings folded, limbs drawn against its body. Its head was turned to one side, beak tucked beneath one wing. Its eyes were closed.

Its furred and feathered side rose, fell softly with each breath. There was blood upon its feathers, its talons rust colored with blood. Its wings looked battered, its fur muddy and wet. It lay still and bedraggled, like a newly pipped hatchling, as though the earth itself had just given it birth.

The formel. Jan started backward again as he realized. This was the formel of the pair that had attacked them—but she was dead! She must be. He himself—they had all seen her plunge out of the sky beyond the lookout knoll, surely to her death? He wondered now, his thoughts spinning. Perhaps she had struggled free of her dead mate at the last moment. Perhaps the drop had not been so great as it had seemed.

All at once a new thought brought him up short: Even his father had been deceived. If Korr had so much as suspected one of the pair had survived, he would have sent warriors to comb the woods and hunt it down. Once again Jan's mind sprinted. If this wingcat were allowed to escape safe home, next storm she might return, bringing others of her kind, well assured how easily they might strike against the prince of the unicorns and live.

Jan eyed the sleeping formel. All thoughts of his self-made exile vanished; his coltish boasts to Dagg vanished as well. The wingcat was three times his size. Alone against her, he had no chance; but if he ran like wildfire, he might just have time to raise the alarm in the Vale and summon the warriors before dusk. Jan backed slowly toward the egress of the cave.

The sun must have moved very slightly in the sky. The light on the cave wall shifted. A ray of red sunlight eased across the gryphon's eye, and Jan felt himself go rigid. The formel stirred, sighing heavily, then coiled herself tighter in her napping ball. Jan in midstep waited, waited, *waited.* The wingcat did not stir again. Jan put his hoof down very carefully and raised the next.

"Jan!"

He started. The voice echoed so loud in the close, oppressive stillness that for a moment he could have sworn it had sounded just beside him.

"Jan!"

He realized then it was a long shout, coming from the outside. Someone was calling him from up the slope. The call came again, nearer this time: Dagg. Dagg had come looking for him. Jan stood frozen in the dusky dimness barely ten paces from the sleeping wingcat. He wished feverishly that his friend would hurry and pass on, give up the search, or else be still.

"Jan!"

This last shout was closer, louder, more insistent. He saw the formel's ears twitch once. Her cat's eye opened slowly, fixing on him—then snapped wide. He felt as if the air had vanished from his throat.

"Jan!"

Dagg's voice had grown impatient, anxious now. The wingcat started up. Jan shied and scrambled back from her, feeling his hindquarters come up hard against the wall. He stared at the gryphon. The gryphon stared at him.

"Come hunting, little princeling?" the gryphon said. "Found me out in my cave just as we found you out in yours, my mate and I."

The formel moved, leaning forward into the sunlight. Her pupils constricted into slits. Jan felt his heart galloping inside his ribs.

"Your father killed my mate not this hour past," she told him quietly, tentatively, cat-and-mouse. "Your father is a mighty warrior, is he not? Kilkeelahr was a mighty warrior as well, among my people, was my mate."

Jan was aware of the hard stone wall pressing his flank and side, of the sweat beneath the long hairs of his coat. Cold fear had begun to numb him.

"But he fell out of favor with the high clans," the formel murmured, singsong, seductively. "Fell out of favor, did my mate. But I dreamed a dream. A white salamander spoke to me. So I proposed this foray, to kill the black prince of the unicorns, and buy our way back into power with glory."

The light of dusk played across the colors of her eyes as she spoke, poured in and among them like water, making them gleam. Gazing into those eyes, Jan felt his mind slacken. It seemed he could see mountains, canyons, many gryphons in the formel's eye. Her voice took on a cutting edge. He hardly noticed.

"Why ever did you *ítichi* come here? Northern plainsdwellers, asking no one's leave to settle. Our leaders have had enough of you; it will not be many years before all the clans are united and Isha grants our prayers for fair winds. Then we will come in a body and harry you out."

The light in the formel's eye shifted and spangled. Jan saw flocks of gryphons swooping and fighting, tearing each other's nests, pashing each other's eggs and carrying off one another's young—things such as he had never seen or heard in ballad or lay.

"Why do you trouble the demesnes of the gryphons? This was *our* land before you stole it."

Around the iris of each of her eyes circled a

narrow band of gold: a thin, bright ring that went round and over, over and round. Jan felt his limbs melting away. There was a serpent in the gryphon's eye, he realized slowly, a snake and a hawk that danced and circled one another. The formel's voice lilted, drifting in and out of his thoughts.

"Your father escaped our plans and cut down my mate. This night the pans will feast on him—on me as well, they would have, had I not torn myself free among the trees. . . . But do not think you will escape *me,* little princeling."

The hawk snatched the snake in its talons. The serpent coiled about the falcon's feet and stung it in the throat. The falcon screamed, clutched at its prize and rose in the air, to carry the serpent, still writhing and stinging, away.

"I have a nest of hungry hatchlings. Do not think you will escape *me*. . . ."

"Jan!"

That other voice cut across his senses like a slap of cold seawater. Jan started, coming to himself. The cave stood narrow and solid about him. The wingcat crouched, eyeing him, and Dagg was calling him from somewhere up the slope.

He heard the formel clucking in frustration as she saw him wake. Only then did he realize what she had been doing—mesmerizing him while she crept close enough to spring. The distance between them had halved. Jan saw the formel's pupils dilate, ruby colored in the flame-colored sunset. She sprang.

Jan dodged, his bad leg giving under him, and

his knees struck the stone floor of the cave. The gryphon shrilled as she missed her strike, coming up hard against the wall. The narrow grotto echoed with her cry. The lunge had taken her past him. Jan skittered to his feet and spun around, vaulting over the staggered gryphon. With a surge of speed he never knew he had, Jan sprinted for the egress of the cave.

BATTLE

Jan bolted for the mouth of the cave, clambering over the heap of fallen earth, and suddenly stopped short. There was nowhere to flee. The ground a pace ahead of him dropped away in a sheer precipice. He caught a flash of green and gold among the tops of the trees below: the dead tercel.

Then he heard a rush in the cave behind him and sprang hard to one side just as the beak of the formel snapped empty air. A narrow goat trail appeared from nowhere, threading the cliffside before him. Jan dashed along it. The gryphon shrieked, scrambling after him, her wings thrashing. He heard her talons scathing the soft, wet rock.

"Jan!"

The cry rang out from the slope above. He saw Dagg standing near the lookout knoll.

"Fly!" Jan shouted. "Dagg, fly!"

Behind him the gryphon screamed and rose into the air. Dagg stood staring, too astonished to move. The goat trail had vanished. Jan threw himself up the steep, rocky slope, the ground crumbling and sliding beneath his hooves. His injured leg wobbled like a dead tree limb.

"Shy!" shouted Dagg.

Jan shied, stumbled, and fell to one side, too late. The formel's talons dug into his shoulders. Jan thrashed wildly. He heard Dagg crying out—alarm or battle yell, he could not tell—as the wingcat hoisted Jan aloft. They hovered just below the hillcrest, almost eye to eye with Dagg.

Jan kicked and twisted, and felt one heel strike home. He kicked again, harder—again. The formel shrieked and snarled, holding him away from her. Then Dagg was charging, rearing, lashing out with his forehooves. The formel pulled back from the hillside, straining to rise.

Jan felt dizzied, as though he had been dancing in circles. His vitals turned. The world below him was sinking, sinking by hoofspans away. Beneath, Dagg yelled, flailing desperately, but the formel had managed to rise beyond his range. Her wings heaved and struggled. Jan's senses swam. He knew beyond all hope that he was lost.

Then another unicorn burst from the trees. She sprang past Dagg, her wild, ringing battle yell snapping Jan back to himself. Tek lunged at the gryphon with head down, her horn aimed. Jan felt the formel tense and twist away as the skewer grazed her side. She writhed.

Tek came to earth. She lost her footing and went down. Dagg charged and leapt, missed, leapt again. Jan glimpsed his friend's unsharpened colt's horn draw blood from the formel's flank. She stamped him hard across the forehead with her lion's paw. Dagg fell to earth, rolling, then staggered to his feet, shaking his head.

Jan twisted in the gryphon's grasp, throwing his head back, trying to bring his own horn into play. He felt it glance across her throat. She screamed again, grappling with his horn, holding him with only one claw now. Her talons grated against his shoulder blades.

Jan felt his head wrenched painfully, and at that moment nearly slipped from her grasp. They fell a few feet in the air, the gryphon trying again to seize him. Jan felt his heels brush the crest of the hill. Tek came charging up the slope and wounded the formel in the shoulder, from behind.

The wingcat staggered in the air, whirling to bat Tek's horn away. Jan pitched forward. His knees struck earth. The gryphon's weight came down and knocked the breath from him. He could not gather his legs beneath him.

"Run!" shouted Tek. At first Jan thought she was talking to him. Then he saw Dagg before him on the hillcrest, blinking at the blood from a long scratch on his forehead. "Away. Give the alarm," Tek was calling. "Go!"

She reared and brought her forehooves down on the fallen gryphon, but was driven back by the great, thrashing wings.

"You're too small to aid me here. Fetch help!" cried Tek. She whirled on Dagg and struck him across the flank with the flat of her horn. "Haste, away!"

Dagg bounded over the hillcrest, shouting the alarm.

The wingcat rose to her hind legs and scrambled to turn. Jan felt himself clutched again; she dragged him with her. As she and Tek faced each other now, the formel began backing away. Tek pursued her, slowly, over the brow of the hill. The young warrior's head was down, her horn ready. The gryphon held Jan between herself and Tek.

The formel edged backward through the trees. Jan caught a glimpse of open space behind. The Vale spread out below them. Dagg's distant cries told him his friend had nearly reached the valley floor. As the gryphon edged toward the end of the trees, Tek feinted and sidled, seeking to drive her back into the wood. But the wingcat screamed, snapping and holding her ground.

The slope opened treeless behind them. Jan felt the formel spring backward once, twice. He was dragged along—and they were airborne again. Jan struggled furiously, for if she got him away from the ground this time, he knew he was lost.

The formel's wings caught an updraft, beating hard. Tek sprang from the hillside, seeming to fly herself for a moment. Jan still thrashed in the gryphon's grasp, but could not break loose. Tek passed beneath them—too low, and cold anguish filled Jan as he realized she had missed her lunge.

Then the wingcat lurched downward suddenly, losing her hold. Her talons tore across his shoulders. He slid free and dropped to the rocky slope. Jan bolted to his feet, wheeling about, and saw Tek skidding downhill with the gryphon's tail caught fast in her teeth.

Tek scrambled to brace herself. She turned, her forelegs splayed, weight thrown back on her hindquarters like a wolf cub playing tug-at-bone. Jan saw her head shaken from side to side, the sinews of her long neck straining, her forehooves lifted from the mountainside as the wingcat fought to flee.

Abruptly, the formel faced about, tearing herself loose. The half-grown mare ducked and dodged. The gryphon struck at her with beak and talons. Eyes half shut against the buffeting of those massive, blue-gold wings, Tek feinted clumsily twice, three times with her horn, but missed each time. Jan saw lines of blood against the pale rose of her neck and shoulders.

He yelled, bounding downslope, and sprang between them. Rearing, he struck the gryphon with hoof and horn. Anger welled in him. Why wouldn't Tek fight? She merely stood, her head bowed, backing slowly downslope while the relentless formel boxed and buffeted her. Jan drove the gryphon back.

"No!" Tek shouted furiously, and shouldered him roughly aside. She snatched the formel in her teeth again, by the wing this time, dragging her forward, past Jan and farther downslope. Below, behind them in the Vale, Jan heard Dagg's alarm cry taken up by other voices.

And he understood then, suddenly. It was a trap, a game. Tek was baiting the gryphon, holding her until the warriors arrived. Jan bounded after the pair of them. If Tek would drag, then he would drive.

He reared and fell on the formel's furred and feathered shoulders. She wheeled, freeing herself from Tek, and struck at him with her great, hooked beak. Jan fell back, feinting at her. He had seen young warriors do that when they sparred.

"Stay back!" Tek shouted. Jan circled downslope, drawing the gryphon after him, toward Tek. "You're too small. You're not a warrior," she cried. "Get behind me. Get back!"

She interposed herself between him and the gryphon. Her backward stepping forced him farther downhill. Too enraged to think of escape, the wingcat lunged after them, screaming and snapping. In the distance behind, he was aware of war cries, the drumming of hooves upon the slope.

"Let me by; let me fight," Jan yelled at Tek. He dodged, trying to slip past her. Tek sidled and kicked at him one-footed to keep him behind.

"You haven't the skill," she snapped, parrying a feint from the formel's claw. She kept herself squarely between the gryphon and Jan. "If she catches you again, she'll carry you off. She can't lift me—stand back! You're in my way. Keep b. . . ."

Her words bit off suddenly. Jan saw a stone skid from under the young mare's heel. She sprawled sideways, head up, her throat exposed. The formel's beak darted, and Jan cried out, vaulting forward before he could even think. He was aware of yelling, keening some terrible war chant.

And suddenly, unicorns, others of his people were surging around him. He glimpsed Tas snorting and plunging, and Leerah his mate. Tek had found her feet again and was fighting like a hillcat. The formel was a fury of screams and talons. Jan saw Dagg charging amid the fray, tearing at the gryphon's wings.

Then someone was rearing, fighting beside him—massy and powerful, blacker than storm. His mighty voice thundered, "Alma, great Alma! Stand at my shoulder, O Mother-of-all!" Other warriors took up the cry. The formel shrilled. The sky above spanned amber and amethyst. The sun in the west was fire.

Jan saw his father rise to stand against the sky, a poultice of chewed medicine wort above his eye now beginning to flake and fall away. A gash. It was only a gash! Jan felt relief flooding his limbs. Korr glanced at him, and Jan saw a gleam he had never seen there before.

His heart lifted, soaring. His aching limbs felt suddenly wondrously strong. Pride, pride lit his sire's eye! He let go a war chant, sang wild and high. He was redeemed. It made him giddy. A deeper trumpet sounded from the prince of the unicorns.

Then it was over, all at once, too suddenly. Jan realized dizzily the fight was done. He came to a halt, and let the careening world around him steady. Unicorns ringed the fallen formel. Fur and feathers lay on the ground.

Dagg stood across from Jan, panting and grinning. His father nearby him pawed the earth gently with one forehoof. Beside him Leerah, pale with dark red dapples, nudged the dead formel with her horn. Tas bent to clean the blood from a nick in his mate's neck.

Jan shook his head and snorted. The fire in his blood had not yet stilled. Tek stood two paces from him, putting no weight on her near foreleg. On the others, Jan saw only a few feather cuts and bruises, a slash or two. He was astonished how unscathed they all were. He ached to the very bone.

Jan turned then to look at his father. The look of approval had not faded from Korr's eye. "Have I not always said," the prince was saying at large, "what a clever colt I sired—to spot the gryphon that got away when none of the rest of us saw? A fighter, too."

The warriors snorted, stamping their assent. Jan's ears burned. Korr was deceived. The prince knew only half the truth. But at that moment, Jan would not have enlightened his sire for all the world. He shook himself. And, if he had not entirely earned his father's goodwill, he was resolved to do so faithfully from this day forward. No more Lawbreaking. He swore it.

More quietly, his father was asking him now, "Are you hale?"

Jan nodded. "Aye." His voice was hoarse from yelling. "And you?"

The prince nodded. "I'll mend. Come, then." He turned, and Jan went beside him. "Teki the healer should see to those cuts."

Jan felt a throbbing in his wounded shoulders then. His side felt bruised. His hurt leg bore his weight only unsteadily. Slowly, he and his father started down the slope. Below them, on the valley floor, Jan saw others waiting. His pale dam, Ses, her round belly heavy and ripe, stood among them.

Glancing back over his shoulder once—he realized then how much his shoulders hurt at the slightest move—Jan saw Tek coming carefully, three-footed, down the slope, flanked by Tas and Dagg. Upslope, he caught sight of Leerah and the rest of the warriors lifting the dead formel onto their shoulders to bear up the hillside and cast over the cliff.

THE LAY OF THE UNICORNS

Each month the unicorns gathered at dusk to dance in a Circle under the full, dusky moon. They were the only race they knew of that did so. For when Alma made the world, she fashioned all the other creatures first, out of earth, wind, water, and air—then invited them to dance. But the pans turned wordless away from her, and the gryphons flew to find mountains to nest in, and the red dragons burrowed deep into the Smoking Hills, and the wyverns laughed.

So Alma created the unicorns after her own shape: sleek-bodied and long-limbed for swift running, wild-hearted and hot-blooded to make them brave warriors. Then she took from the cycling moon some of its shining stuff to fashion their hooves and horns and make them dancers. So the last-born and best-beloved of Alma called themselves also the moon's children, and each month danced the ringdance under the round, rising moon.

Equinox fell on the night of the full moon that

spring. Jan stretched out beneath its pale, smoke light falling from among a river of stars. The ground beneath him was springy soft and thawing with the year. His shaggy winter coat, not yet begun to shed, kept out the coolness. He stretched his limbs among the fine shoots of new grass that threaded amid the old.

Lifting his head from his knees, he gazed at the other unicorns assembled in the wide, rough Circle on the valley floor. Some were standing lazily, three-footed, regaining their breath. Others bowed their heads to nibble the new grass. Murmurs of talk and nickers of laughter drifted on the still night air. The moon had risen a quarter of the way toward its zenith, and the dancing was over now.

Jan lay inside the Circle with the other initiates. He gave Dagg beside him a nudge with his hind heel, murmuring, "Wake," for on the low rise jutting near them at the Circle's heart, Khraa the king had gotten to his feet. The tales were about to start.

Jan's grandsire was old and did not seem it. Strong-built like his heir, but leaner, Khraa stood upon the ledge, pale gray as cloudcover, with a coal-dark mane and hooves. He was the king, and would have ruled the unicorns in a time of peace. Even now he retained his place as high justice, head of all ceremonies save those of battle, and would rule as regent during the coming absence of his son.

But Korr the prince led the unicorns now, for

the children-of-the-moon were at war, and had been at war for four hundred years.

"O unicorns," cried Khraa the king, "here we stand under the rising moon, midwiving in the birth of the new year with our dances and our songs. The dancing, it is done, and the singing is to come. On the morrow's morn, our young fillies, our young colts will slip away unseen upon their Pilgrimage through the dark Pan Woods, over the Great Grass Plain, and across the crumbling shelf-land of the sleeping wyverns—let them not wake—until they come upon the Mirror of the Moon, our sacred well, there to perform their rite of passage."

The gray king paused, drawing breath. All the unicorns had lain down now. Night stretched dark and bright around them. Jan listened to the king.

"The time has come," he said, "for singing the Lay of the Unicorns, which tells of the beginning of this war and how our race was driven from its territories by treachery and forced to abandon the Moon's Mere—long, it was a long time past. Singer, come forth! Let the story be sung."

Khraa slipped silently from the ledge then and lay down beside his mate. Jan spotted the healer lying within the Circle. Even by moonlight he could make out the great black patches patterning the other's white coat, the dark spot encircling each eye so they stood out huge and seemed never to blink. But the one who rose from the grass at the king's nod was not Teki, but another lying beside him.

"Who is it?" whispered Dagg.

The young mare mounted the rise, her black and rose coloring pale ghostly under the moon. Jan hardly recognized her at first. It had been nearly a half-month since the battle of the gryphons—his shoulders were healed—and he had not seen Tek, save in far glimpses, since then. He had not realized before this that the healer's daughter was a singer of tales.

"Hail," she cried out, her voice low, harsh-sweet, "I'll sing you a tale of when Halla was princess of the unicorns, and a rare princess was she. This was while her father Jared was yet alive and king, and in the time when queen or king still ruled the unicorns.

"And this was long after the great Serpent-clouds had scoured the Plain. And this was some after the war with the haunts had been fought and won. And this was just after the spring fevers had carried off Halla's first mate, and her two younglings, a twin filly and foal—but before she had taken Zod the singer to husband as her second mate, while the unicorns still lived in the Hallow Hills by the sacred well, in and around the milkwood groves that now are called the Wyvern Wood. Because of the things I shall tell of in this tale. Because of the coming of the wyrms."

"What's milkwood?" murmured Jan, to himself. He had never wondered it before.

"Hist," Dagg told him. "I want to hear."

Tek changed her stance a little on the rocky platform, facing now a slightly different quarter of the Circle.

"It was summer, midsummer, the solstice," she sang, "and winter a long time gone. But winter touched the hearts of the unicorns still, for the herd was shrunk and saddened at the death of so many fine warriors and weanlings, the young with the old, from a spring plague that year, the princess's own nurselings among them. Zod the singer was just coming into the full glory of his voice, and aging Jared, Halla's father, was king.

"Then Halla, dawn-colored like fire, stood beside the moon's pool, sad in contemplation, asking Alma why That One had seen fit to steal away the flower of the unicorns."

Jan felt another wondering. "What's fire?" he said aloud.

"I don't know," hissed Dagg. "It comes from lightning, or maybe the sun."

Tek had paused a moment in her song.

"Hot," murmured Jan, "so the ballads say. It dances and darts." He had heard of fire every now and again, in story and song. Fire dwelled in dragons' mouths. This or that hero was color-of-fire. But Jan had never seen any, and no unicorn he knew had ever seen any. "What is it, I wonder. Is it alive?"

"Be still now," Dagg insisted. "I want to listen."

Above them on the rise, under the moon, Tek had changed her stance again, turned just a little.

Such was the singing of the unicorns. Jan knew that by the time the tale was done, she would have turned full Circle and taken in the whole Ring of listeners.

"Halla the princess stood at the wellside, when of a sudden she glimpsed movement across the water, some creature emerging from the green, cool woods bordering the Mere. It was a pale thing, like a great snake or a salamander, and came sliding out of the forest, lean and wrinkled as a dying toad. Watching, she saw it dip its long neck to the water to drink.

" 'Stop,' Halla cried, before its narrow snout could touch the surface and disturb the stillness of that hallowed pool.

"The creature looked up across the water with its clear, uncolored eyes. It seemed unable to see her well.

" 'This is a sacred place,' Halla informed it. 'Only we, the children-of-the-moon, may drink here.'

"Then the thing flicked its thin, forked tongue very fast between its needle teeth, as in anger. But in a moment, eyeing the dawn-colored princess of the unicorns, it grew softer, seeming to reconsider. It spoke to her in a strange sliding voice that hissed and lilted, hollow and velvety sharp. 'Oh, please, a drink. One drink. I perish.'

" 'Not of this lake,' the king's daughter replied. 'But if you thirst, I will tell you where lies another pool whereof you may drink.' "

Again Tek turned away from him and Dagg,

more toward the side as she gazed over the Circle.

"And at those words," the healer's daughter sang, "at Halla's words, the creature at the wellside crumpled, seeming too weak to rise. So Halla walked along the curve of the shore until she came to it and bade it follow. It roused itself with difficulty and came slithering alongside her downslope through the woods.

"She studied it as they went, long and pale as a fish's belly, cold-looking like ice. It seemed smaller in body than a unicorn, with a long, scaled tail that had a sting-barb at its end. It kept two stubby forelegs folded against its body as it slithered. High on its neck, behind the head, a ruff of gills fanned and gaped when it opened its mouth. Its teeth were long, back-curving fangs.

" 'What are you?' Halla asked it.

" 'Oh, please,' it panted. 'Water first. A little water.'

"They reached the second pool. Near the top of a fall of stone shelves, a little spring welled and cascaded forming a pool at the base of the rocks. As soon as the pale creature saw this, it darted past Halla quick as a grass-flick and dropped its long neck to the water, lapping at it and laving it over its head.

"And as it drank, it seemed to grow, its withered sides swelling like a toad that is fat with poison. Then it slipped into the water and writhed about, bathing and whining a high, thin pleasure-song—until it caught sight of Halla on the bank and crept out of the pool, cringing again.

" 'You must forgive me,' it moaned. 'It has been months since I last tasted water.' It was now nearly twice the size it had been before.

" 'What are you?' Halla asked again.

" 'I?' it said, in its strange, sliding voice, preening its wet, gleaming skin. 'I am Lynex, and a wyvern.' "

Jan listened to the singer's voice, clear and dusky under the smoke moonlight. The wyverns were a noxious breed, sprung from the stink of quagmires at the beginning of the world. That was why the unicorns had come to call them 'wyrms': slithery, slippery things. Tek sang:

"But just at that moment, as he was speaking, the wyrm caught sight of the caves and rock shelves beyond the pool, spreading away to the southeast. Streams threaded across those rocks, welling and falling, pale as cloud. And seeing these, the wyvern gave out little sharp barks of glee, sliding here and there over the shelves, muttering.

" 'Ah, but these are just the thing. They would suit perfectly! Not as vast as the dens we left, but we could dig more at need. Perhaps . . . .' Then he turned on the princess of the unicorns, demanding, 'Who dwells here?'

" 'No one,' replied Halla, mildly.

" 'Ah.' The wyvern sat, considering.

" 'But these lands fall within our territory,' the princess said, 'the unicorns'.'

"The creature glanced at her. 'Quite so,' it answered, more softly now. 'Quite so. I . . . we . . . that is, my people . . . .'

" 'Your people?' Halla inquired.

" 'There are more—a very few. A very few more of us. We have been lost, wandering across the Plain. We wish to settle.'

" 'You seek the unicorns' leave to settle here?'

"The wyvern bowed stiffly down to the dust. 'You would know our gratitude.'

" 'I have not the right either to grant you or to turn you away,' Halla replied. 'My father Jared is king. Tell your leaders to assemble here tomorrow. Bathe and drink. I will bid the elders of the unicorns come to you. Then we will decide.'

"So Halla left the wyrm beside the shelves and pools, and sprang off through the milkwood trees, traversing meadow and dale and grove to gather the unicorns to come parley with the wyrms."

Tek fell silent in her singing, bowing her head. She changed her stance again, turning more and more away from Jan, taking in others of the Circle. He was aware of Dagg beside him in the dark.

"I wonder . . ." he began, but his friend's sigh cut him short.

"That's your trouble," Dagg whispered. "You're always *wondering*. Now quiet. She's starting the second cant."

Tek lifted her head. "And next day beside the shelves and pools, parley was held between the sinuous leader of the wyverns and Jared the old king, with Halla his daughter and Zod the singer and a great many others, both wyverns and unicorns, present as well.

" 'How many have you in your band?' inquired Jared of the wyrms.

" 'Not many,' Lynex replied, hollow-voiced and sliding. 'Only a very few. Not nearly enough to fill these burrows.'

" 'He is lying,' murmured Halla between her teeth, close to her father's ear. 'I sent scouts to spy them out. They reported more than just a few. Yet most, they said, were torpid, near death. They look a livelier lot this day. Well-watered.'

" 'We do not wish to intrude,' the wyvern leader continued, 'only leave to stay here a little and rest from our arduous journey.'

" 'When first you spoke with me,' said Halla, stepping forward, 'you said you desired to settle.'

" 'Only for a season or two,' Lynex replied, 'to breed. We must have hatching grounds to brood our eggs.'

" 'Well enough,' said Jared, seemingly very little intent upon the parley. He had slept but fitfully the night before, strange troubles sliding through his dreams, and he was old, grown old before his time—sometimes his mind wandered; no one could say why.

" 'I see a wyvern breeding in a unicorn's belly,' said Zod then softly, an evening-blue unicorn all spattered with milk, 'eating up the children that were there.'

"But the princess ignored his words, for he

spoke but softly, near her ear. Zod was a seer of visions and a dreamer of dreams, and often spoke riddles that meant nothing.

" 'How long will it take your eggs to hatch, and how long thereafter before your young may travel?' said Halla to the wyrm.

" 'Not long,' said Lynex, preening his supple skin with a thin, forked tongue.

" 'Well enough,' the king replied.

" '*Not* well enough,' the princess cried. 'How long?'

" 'Oh, a season,' said Lynex, smiling. 'No more than that. Our young thrive fast.'

" 'How many eggs do your kind lay in a clutch?'

" 'Oh, two—three?' the wyrm replied, as if he did not know. As if he were asking her.

" 'No snake I know lays so few little death-beads at one squat,' muttered Zod the singer, more loudly.

" 'We are not snakes,' the wyvern snapped, fanning his hood. A double tongue flicked angrily between his needle teeth. 'We are wyverns.'

" 'Wyrms.'

" 'Peace, Zod,' said Jared the king; then, to the creatures: 'Pay him no heed. We do not. He is a speaker of foolish nothing.'

" 'Wise foolish nothing,' the seer replied beneath his breath."

"Why don't they believe him?" muttered Jan under his own breath now. He could never lie still during the second cant. "Why doesn't the princess heed him—can't she see the wyverns are lying?"

"This is a tale," Dagg hissed at him. "Of course *we* can tell."

"Halla spoke," said Tek. " 'Where will you go when your younglings are ready?' the princess of the unicorns inquired.

"The wyrm hung its head. 'We do not know. We will move on, across the Great Grass Plain, hoping to stumble upon someplace hospitable to our kind, where we might live peaceably, disturbing no one.' "

"Liar," muttered Jan.

"Be *still*," hissed Dagg.

" 'Whence do you come?' said Halla to the wyverns. 'Why have you journeyed across the Plain?'

" 'Ah,' cried Lynex, 'we come from the north, the north and east where once we dwelled in harmony with our cousins, the red dragons. But our cousins cast us off—for envy, we think. We are too beautiful for their liking, though that is not the reason they would give.'

"The wyvern's eyes reddened with rancor.

" 'They said we were too many; they said . . . .' He stopped himself suddenly. 'Ah, but . . . as you see, we are only a very few.'

"Halla stood gazing out over the backs of the wyverns. She swatted a deerfly on her haunch and picked testily at the ground with one forehoof. Now that she scanned, she saw the white wyrms matched the diminished herd of the unicorns nearly beast for beast. 'Not so few,' she muttered to herself.

" 'More than that,' her scout beside her murmured. 'Our lookouts spotted many more than that.'

" 'Are all your people here assembled?' Halla asked aloud.

" 'All that yet are left to us alive,' Lynex replied.

" 'Well enough,' Jared replied. Then turning to Halla and her advisors, he said—seemingly to them, but loud enough for the wyrms to hear—'Harmless enough, they seem. I say we should succor them.'

" 'A moment, father,' the princess cried. 'They appear to me less harmless than you think.' She turned again to the drove of wyverns. 'What do you eat?'

"And at this, for the first time, the wyverns did not answer at once, but turned to consult among themselves in their soft, sliding whispers.

" 'Fish,' said Lynex, turning, 'when we can get them, small lizards, birds' eggs. But when those cannot be found, we may subsist on grass for a little, as we have done these past months—that same sweet grass which you yourselves eat.'

"Halla eyed their needle teeth.

" 'Aye, fine sharp cusps they have,' murmured Zod the singer, 'for the grinding of grass.'

" 'You have poison stings on your tails," said Halla.

"Then the wyverns flicked their tails and hissed till Lynex stilled them. 'Mere decoration only,' he replied, brandishing the barbed tip of his tail. 'And no defense against dragons, I fear.'

" 'Then why . . .' the princess began.

" 'Well enough, well enough!' her father cried. 'Let us put an end to this bickering. It grows late, and I am weary.' Before his daughter could protest he continued: 'Hear my judgment. Let the wyverns make dens in the rocks for one season. At the end of that time let us assemble again to parley their further stay.'

"Then Lynex the wyvern king bellied down to the dust. 'You will not regret this largess, O king. We are used to living inconspicuously; we will not disturb you—and we sleep all winter.'

"Coming forward then, he and Jared sealed their bargain with the pledge-kiss rulers give one another. But as her father turned away, Halla saw that the ear above the cheek where the wyvern king had kissed him lay crumpled, stood upright no more.

"Then the wyverns gave a great hissing shout and disappeared quick as a twitch into every burrow and cranny and cave in the rocks, so that at the end of ten heartbeats there was not tip nor tail to be seen of them, nor hardly any sign that they had been there at all.

" 'And now that they are slithered in,' said Zod to no one, softly, 'how ever shall we get them out again?'

"And Halla said quietly to her scout beside her, 'Let us send runners over Alma's back to north and east to find the red dragons. I would know what reason *they* give for the casting out of these slithery cousins of theirs.' "

Tek paused again and bowed her head. The second cant was done. She stood facing wholly away from Jan and Dagg now, gazing out over the far half of the Circle. The moon had floated well up into the sky, its cool light spilling as pale as water.

"So the runners were sent," chanted Tek from her ledge. Jan heard the faintest echo of her words bounding back from the far hillside. ". . . at Halla's behest and without the king's knowing. Summer paled slowly into autumn, and hardly a scale was seen of the wyverns. They kept to their rock shelves, to themselves, until the unicorns nearly forgot their presence with the feasting and the dancing and the gathering of fall.

"But Halla was troubled. Her messengers did not return, and it seemed that her father made merrier than the rest, strange merriment. His thoughts strayed and rambled. And the ear where the wyvern had kissed him still drooped, so that now he was a little deaf. It uneased her.

"Zod, too, seemed uneasy. Haunting were the lays, all danger and betrayal, that fell from his tongue, mostly for her ears, though the princess did not know him well. And when on cold autumn nights from beneath some spreading fir Halla awoke to a distant, mournful cry, she knew it was the singer at his dreams.

"Winter came, and with it, snow. The well-springs froze, and then no sight or sound of the wyverns came. They lay curled tight in sleeping knots below ground, so the unicorns supposed—though sometimes wisps of acrid mist rose from the airholes to their dens. It was a puzzle passing strange. No one could make it out.

"Then the unicorns ate of their stores, pawing through the snow to find forage, and chewed the leaves of spruce and fir, warm in their winter shag, thinking nothing of the wyrms—while Zod sang songs of doom all winter and Halla waited for her runners to return."

Tek had turned just past halfway around in her circling. Jan began to be able to see her face again, though she faced still toward the far side of the Circle. The lightest of echoes sang back from the distant slope as she chanted, shadowing her words. The moon hung two-thirds of the way to its zenith. Jan listened to Tek's singing under the moon.

"Spring came. The snows dissolved. Ice that had locked the pools melted, and new grass sprang upon the Plain. Then two young colts disappeared within a day of one another and were not seen again. Searchers combed diligently, but no trace could be found.

"Companions said they had last seen them in the south and east, near the wyvern cliffs, but no sign of wyverns either could be found, and no answer came when the searchers shouted down into their caves. Jared the king said the year was early yet for wyrms to be abroad. No more was said. No more could be done.

"Then a young mare heavy in foal went up to the Mirror of the Moon to bear, but returned not, nor her companion the midwife. They were not seen again. This time the searchers found wyvern tracks and belly marks about the poolside and crystalized droppings under the trees. But still no answer came from beneath the shelves when the searchers called, and no wyverns emerged.

"Jared the king said still the white wyrms were asleep, fast slumbering, and the searchers must have mistook the signs, that the tracks must be those of banded pards, or other grasscats wandered in from the Plain. But when urged by his advisors, he would post no lookouts. So scouts were posted at Halla's word, against the orders of the king.

"Soon some of them said they had seen wyverns moving about the shelves at night. Others spoke of wyverns bathing in the sacred Mirror of the Moon before dawn. Hearing this, the princess grew alarmed, and ordered mineral salt thrown down about the Mere to keep them off.

"But when clear traces were found at last that the wyverns had visited the salt-clay cliffs where the dead are laid beneath the stars and had carried off the bodies of warriors put to rest there, Halla went with this knowledge to her father and confronted him before his counselors."

Tek had turned more around now. The faint, silvery echo still repeated her words.

"At first Jared laughed at his daughter's charges against the wyrms. Then he grew angry when she told him of the watchers she had posted against his word. And suddenly, without warning, he cried out in a voice that seemed unlike his own:

" 'Traitor, traitor, thrice a traitor! My own daughter, my heir, has betrayed me!'

"He got no further, for by this time a great assembly had gathered, and hearing that Halla had set sentries upon the white wyrms, most of the people cried out in her favor, for there was much murmuring now against the wyverns, and much fear.

"But even as they were speaking, a messenger came galloping, tangle-hooved and exhausted. He pitched to a halt before Halla, bowing low.

" 'Hail, princess. I have returned from the red dragons. All summer it took us to find their country across the Plain, and all autumn to persuade them we were not spies. Over the winter, one of our number died, and two are still held hostage. But the dragons have allowed me to return to you, and here is the answer to the question we carried:

“ ‘The red dragons cast out the wyverns from the Smoking Hills in wintertime and drove them away across the Great Grass Plain, hoping to spell their death. The wyrms had been let live among their hosts as scavengers and carrion clearers. The dragons claim no kinship to them.

“ ‘But when the wyverns began to breed out of hand and grow past a moderate size, and carry off dragon pups to devour, and rob the earthen tombs—the firedrakes bury their dead in the earth—then the dragons set snares and caught them at their plunder, fell on them and drove them from their burrows with fire.

“ ‘But Lynex, the wyrms’ leader, and some others escaped them. The dragons let them go, thinking surely upon the Great Grass Plain they would die. But Méllintéllinas, who is queen of the red dragons, warns you, Halla, princess of the moon’s children, that this Lynex is as subtle as craft and she believes, though she cannot be certain, that he has stolen from their godstone a golden carrying bowl, and in it, the secret of their fire.’ ”

A bowl. Jan wondered what a carrying bowl could be. He had never wondered it before. He drew breath to speak then, but Dagg beside him in the darkness murmured, “List.”

The healer’s daughter had turned in her Circle under the moon. The soft songshadow still repeated her words.

“Hearing these things of the wyverns, the unicorns cried out in consternation, but Jared shouted them down. ‘Let be! Let them be. Why should we trouble the wyrms? They have done us no harm, caused us no alarm. . . .’

“ ‘They have stolen our children,’ cried Halla, ‘both the born and the unborn, and our people, and our dead. They have drunk of the well of the unicorns, and hide in their holes when we call them to task.’

“ ‘Lies,’ cried the king, ‘all lies by your followers to unseat me. I know who the true friends of the unicorns are. You have defied me! You have moved in secret against me. Now this messenger of yours brings more lies.’

“ ‘There is a worm in his brain,’ chanted Zod, low like a dirge. ‘I have seen it in a dream, and it eats away his reason.’

“ ‘You traitor,’ Jared cried, broken-eared, deaf—and his words still tumbled out in that strange hollow voice unlike his own. ‘Usurper. No longer my daughter. Death for what you have done to me! You shall die.’

“And before another unicorn could utter a word or draw a breath, Jared the king reared with hooves and horn poised to strike down the princess of the unicorns. But Halla fended him off, though all unwillingly. She smote him a great blow to the breast with her forehooves and struck him with the flat of her horn to the skull.

“Then the king went down, unexpectedly, to everyone’s surprise. He fell like one shot through with poison, and lay at the unicorns’ feet, stone dead. Those assembled watched his wilted ear twitch once, twice, and a tiny wyvern crawled forth, long as a foreshank and fat with its feasting. Its forked tongue flickered between needle teeth.

"Halla cried out and rose up to smash the murdering thing with her hooves, but Zod the singer sprang between them, crying, 'Beware, princess. Even newborn, it carries death in its tail. Its spittle is sweet poison on teeth sharp as fishbones, and its breath is a bringer of nightmares. I know; I have seen it, I who dream dreams.'

"But even as he was speaking, a cry went up in the south and east, from scouts flying to bring the alarm:

" 'The wyverns, the wyverns—to war!' "

Above the Vale, the full moon floated, serenely bright, nearing its zenith. Tek stood in perfect profile now, her voice pitched to carry; she sang out like a bell:

"All about the gathered unicorns, the wyverns now came streaming, slithering like flood rain—many more than there had been at midsummer, many more than the unicorns were. Most of them were little things, no bigger than hatchlings. Quick as kestrels, lithe as eels, they darted about the heels of the unicorns, stinging.

"And snaking at the head of them, Lynex shouted, 'Ah-ha! Ah-ha! Did I not say our younglings thrive fast? Come, prit; come, pet.'

"Then the wyrmlet that had crawled from the dead king's ear flashed to the wyvern king and twined about his neck. And seeing this, Halla rose up, shouting a war cry. Her warriors rallied. The unicorns charged. All day the fighting lasted. Many wyverns were slain, the great ones pierced through the vitals, the little ones trampled underfoot.

"But the warriors were scattered and few. Some were yet heavy in foal or only recently delivered. Many shattered their horns against the wyverns' breasts, for the wyrms were made with a bony plate under the skin and above the heart that could not be pierced. And those that had been stung felt a langor overtaking them, till they sank to the ground, unable to rise."

Jan squirmed in the dark in his place beside Dagg. He champed his teeth, hardly able to bear that Alma should grant all things in season—even defeat for the unicorns. The singer sang:

"Slow and by little, the unicorns fell back, and the wyverns poured after them in fierce hordes until the westering sun hung like a gryphon's eye, and the unicorns fought upon the last slope of the Hallow Hills, upon the verges of the Plain.

"Halla cried out then, 'Is all lost? Hoof and horn prove no match to the barbs of the wyrms. So many lie slain. Another hour and we shall all of us be dead. Is no hope left?'

" 'One hope,' answered Zod, the singer of dreams, for still he fought alongside her, protecting her flank. 'Fly—away across the Great Grass Plain. These wyrms will gorge themselves upon our dead and theirs, and will not follow.'

" 'Run?' Halla cried, staring at him. 'Leave the

Mirror of the Moon for them to lap and paddle in?'

" 'The Moon's Mere is now bitter salt,' the seer said, 'and poison to them. You have said yourself, O princess, another hour's fight will see us dead. Better for us to fly now and live, to grow many and strong again, one day to return and reclaim our land—than to die to the last here and now, giving it up to them forever.' "

Jan kicked one leg in silent protest. His young heart cried out, *No. Better to die, die fighting to the last, than to live with the shame.* But that was foal's talk, and he knew it, that no warrior would countenance. The healer's daughter turned some and spoke, soft echoes shadowing her speech:

" 'But how may we ever reclaim it?' cried Halla, like one dying for grief. 'How long must we wait?'

"Then her companion's eyes grew far and strange. 'I have heard in dreams,' so the seer said, 'that it will not come in our lifetime. Our sons will not see it, nor our sons' daughters. But when at last the night-dark one shall be born among the unicorns, then the Mirror of the Moon will grow sweet again, and the wyverns shall perish in fire. Our people shall call him the Firebringer: a great warrior as are you, O princess, and a seer of dreams as am I.' "

"How does he know that?" muttered Jan, hardly realizing he spoke.

"Seers know things," whispered Dagg. "Alma tells them, and they know."

 Tek stood now as she had at the tale's beginning, and the moon hung above her at zenith in the sky. And it seemed to Jan, as he lay listening, that that soft songshadow, faint on the very verge of his hearing, still sounded from before him, from the far hillside, though the healer's daughter now faced wholly away from that slope as she sang.

"So Halla, hearing the dreamer's words, ate at last the bitter root of defeat, bowing to the wisdom of the moon, which says that all things wax and wane, even the greatness of the unicorns. She bade her warriors escape and save themselves, flee away into the dusk while the wyverns in the foothills sat howling their glee.

"But glancing back, Halla—the very last to leave the field—saw Lynex holding aloft in his teeth the bough of a tree all ablaze with amber flowers. Beside him upon the ground rested a golden bowl of glowing stones.

" 'What, fly, will you?' cried the wyrm king through his teeth. 'Then let this pursue you in our stead. Never think to trouble us again, vile unicorns!'

"Then he cast the scarlet brand upon the Plain, and where it came to earth, suddenly the stubgrass bloomed as well with wisps of light that danced and ran before the wind. Clouds of choking dust arose beneath the fury of their passing, and they left the grass behind them blackened in curling crisps.

"Those whom the hot, darting dancers touched screamed wild in pain. Not horn nor hoof availed against them, and any who fled slow or wounded, the flames ran down like pards upon the Plain. The unicorns fled rampant then, terrified, for two whole nights and a day, till spring storms trampled out the deadly flares, and the children-of-the-moon dropped where they stood, to sleep like dead things in the rain."

The healer's daughter fell silent then, and her echo fell instantly silent as well. Very like her own voice it was, only a little deeper. Jan sighed heavily, studying the ground. The story always ended the same, with the rout of the unicorns. If only . . . . He screwed his knees tighter into the turf. If only, if only—he knew not what. Tek made an ending to the tale:

I have sung you the Lay of the Unicorns, how we were cast from our lands by wyverns and wandered many seasons, south over the Plain, till at last we came upon a Vale. And here, by Alma's grace, we have begun to grow strong again.

"But we have never forgotten that these are not our own true lands. One day we shall regain the Hallow Hills. Each year some of us must return: quiet, careful, on dangerous Pilgrimage, to drink that drink which makes us what we are, unicorns, warriors, children-of-the-moon.

"The sacred well, the Hallow Hills, are not yet ours again. The Firebringer is not among us yet, but he is coming. He is coming—soon."

Tek stood a moment on the ledge and then descended. Those in the Circle began to stir. Dagg in the moonlit dark beside Jan whispered, "She changed that last."

Jan was still gazing after Tek as she lay down beside her father now.

"She didn't just say the Firebringer was coming. She said he was coming soon."

Jan nodded absently, thinking of something else. "I wonder," he murmured. "Did this valley belong to anyone before we came here?"

Dagg eyed him with a frown. "It was empty. Everyone knows that."

"I wonder," murmured Jan. "Someone told me once . . . it seems . . . ."

This valley was ours before you stole it. Ever since the day of the gryphons, those words had been in his mind. Who was it that had told him that? Every time he strove to picture the speaker, the image slipped from him. It was like a dream he had awakened from and now could not recall.

Khraa upon the ledge had begun to speak, but Jan hardly listened, still trying to puzzle out those strange, half-remembered words: *This valley was ours. . . .*

Dagg was nudging him. "Do you think she's a dreamer? Tek, I mean. Maybe she's foreseen the Firebringer."

Jan felt his skin prickle. For a moment the thought quickened his blood: that the Firebringer might be more than just an old legend, that the prophecy might one day come to pass.

"But do you think," whispered Dagg, bending closer, "she could have meant Korr?"

Jan started and stared at his friend. The feeling of exhilaration passed. The prince's son snorted and shook his head. "Zod foretold 'a seer of dreams.' "

"Yes, but the dreaming sight doesn't always come early," said Dagg. "And your father's coat *is* color-of-night."

Jan looked away. Could that be—his sire, the Firebringer? The idea unsettled him somehow. True, Korr was black and a great warrior, the first black prince in all the history of the unicorns. But his father had no use for dreamers and their dreams. He would have no truck with them at all—except that once with Jah-lila, the healer's mate, who lived outside the Vale.

Jan snorted again. No, it could never be Korr. Impossible! He rolled onto his back and scrubbed himself against the soft, grass-grown dirt. His winter coat was still long and shaggy from the cold months, and he wished it would shed. Spring was early this year, and it itched.

He shook himself then, and settled himself. Dagg beside him had closed his eyes. The gray king had quit the ledge, and all around, Jan heard other unicorns preparing for sleep. He let his breath out slowly; his eyelids drooped.

Above him the moon, mottled and bright, fissured down its middle like a ripe eggshell. Out of it crawled a winged serpent that hung above him in the starry sky, breathing a sour breath upon him and speaking words he could not understand.

Jan's limbs twitched in his sleep; his nostrils flared. Breath caught and shuddered in his throat. Dagg jostled beside him in the dark. Jan rolled onto his other side and breathed more deeply then. His eyelids ceased to flutter. The snake in the heavens flew away.

It was very late. He realized he must have slept, but he could not remember having closed his eyes. The unbroken moon, whole and undamaged, had tilted a little way down from its zenith. Jan saw a figure standing among the sleeping unicorns.

It turned away, walking toward the Circle's edge, then it sprang lightly over a sleeper and cantered noiselessly toward the far hillside. Jan felt the drumming of heels through the ground and lay wondering. By Law, no one was allowed to break the Circle until the moon was down.

As the figure disappeared upslope into the trees, Jan realized suddenly that it seemed to be heading toward that point whence the echo had come while Tek had been singing. He frowned, shaking his head. The valley stood empty now, the Circle around him still and undisturbed.

It's restlessness, he told himself. *I imagined it.* He felt no drum of heels in the soft earth now. He shut his eyes, shivering with fatigue. And as he slipped again into that country between waking and sleep, it seemed the night air brought to him, just for a moment, a delicious odor like roses in summer. He slept deep without dreams then, till morning.

THE PAN WOODS

The trees leaned close around them as they walked, and bird cries haunted through the gloom. The air was cool, with gray jays and redwings flashing through the wells of light. As Jan watched, golden foxes slunk through the bracken. There a hare crouched, its eyes as black as river stones, beside a skeletal thicket all budded in yellow-green. Deer browsed among the shadows, raising their heads as the unicorns passed, gazing after the newcomers with great, uncurious eyes.

The pilgrims slipped through the still Pan Woods that forested the folded hills as far as the Plain, a day's journey to the west. They had risen at dawn, all those within the Circle, sprung up and shaken the sleep from them, while those forming the Ring around them had lain sleeping still. At a nod from the prince, the initiates had turned, leapt over the sleepers, and stolen from the valley—silently, lest any left behind awaken, breaking the Circle before the pilgrims were away.

They moved in single file now, the colts and fillies behind the prince and flanked by warriors here and there. Over the long train of backs wending before him, Jan caught glimpses of rose and black, the healer's daughter, and sometimes white and black, her sire. Others he remembered from the battle of the gryphons, for Korr chose only the worthiest warriors to accompany the initiates over the Plain.

The Hallow Hills lay far to northward, a half month's running. By then the full moon that had set over the Vale a half hour gone would be dwindled to nothing. By the moon's dark, then, while the wyverns slept, the unicorns would keep Vigil beside the sacred Mere; and at daybreak they would dip their hooves and horns and drink a single sip of its bitter waters.

So much Jan knew of the ceremony at their journey's end. So much and no more. He and Dagg filed on through the trees of the Pan Woods, near the tail of the line. And the morning passed.

They halted near noon to lie up beside a tangle of berry brush. Splendid curtains of sun streamed into a small clearing nearby. Jan and Dagg threw themselves down upon the soft brown carpet of bracken leaf, near the clearing's edge but out of the light, and lay there, not talking. The morning's long walk had tired them.

When Alma first had made the world, so the singers said, she had offered her children the gift of speech. The unicorns took it gladly, and sang their thanks to her. The gryphons took it, and the dragons, even the wyrms. But the goatling pans ran away into the woods, hiding themselves from the Mother-of-all, refusing her gift. And for that, the unicorns despised them.

Jan and Dagg had even seen one once, a pan—a small, cowardly thing. The previous summer they had stolen high upon the slopes, looking for red rueberries to roll in so that, returning to their companions below, they might game them into believing they had been sprung upon by bobtailed hillcats.

But unexpectedly, they had come upon a strange beast: round-headed, flat-faced, and horned like a goat. Its hairless chest was broad and shallow, with a bluish hide, its forelimbs fingered like birds' feet, and the hind limbs shaggy brown with cloven heels. A slight figure, it would have stood only shoulder high to Korr.

It had been crouching when they had come upon it, plucking ripe berries from the ruebush with the long toes of its forelegs; but it had sprung up and dashed away when it saw them, upon its hind limbs alone, like a wingless bird. He and Dagg had chased it, but it had disappeared over the hillcrest and down into the Pan Woods quick as cunning. What an odd, ungainly looking creature. Ugly as old bones.

Remembering, Jan smiled with the easy arrogance of unicorns and nibbled the young buds from the briar beside him. It was Alma's frown upon the goatlings that made them so. Only her favored ones, the moon's children, walked truly in beauty. He swatted at a deerfly that lighted on his rump. The shoots of the bush tasted tender and green.

The handful of warriors stood guard about the dozing initiates, or moved silently among the trees, scouting for pans. Jan watched them idly, and presently he heard a strange sound far in the distance, drawn out and windy, like the whooping of herons. It died down after a few moments, then began again, nearer. And as he listened, it seemed to Jan he could discern a pattern in the cries, calling and replying to one another through the trees.

Dagg was just turning to him, drawing breath to speak, when all at once Jan cut him off with a hiss. He nodded. Teki and another warrior had emerged from the trees a dozen paces from them and stood conferring with the prince.

"Something's afoot," murmured Jan, feeling his blood quickening. "Maybe they've spotted pans."

All morning since they had left the Vale, he had been half hoping they might stumble upon the pans. They were not colts anymore, after all. They had nothing to fear. Indeed, it would be a fine game, putting a few of those timid little blueskins to flight. The Woods had been so quiet, the morning so monotonous, with only bird cries for distraction. Boredom nibbled at Jan with tiny, needle teeth.

"It *is* pans," whispered Dagg. "It must be."

The two warriors had broken off from Korr now and were whistling the initiates to be up and off. Jan sprang to his feet and shook himself, laughing with Dagg at the prospect of diversion. The file forming behind Teki was already trotting away into the trees.

"Step brisk," Jan heard Korr calling, "and less noise."

Jan champed his tongue and hurried into line. Dagg behind him was doing the same. Since the day of the gryphons, Jan had kept his vow, following the prince's word always, at once, without questions. His father's goodwill was too precious, had come too dearly bought to part with now. Jan swallowed his high spirits and stepped brisk.

The gloom of the Pan Woods enfolded them. Behind them, Korr was bringing up the rear of the train. Jan pricked his ears, scanning the trees. Nothing. The Woods were empty, still. He lifted his head, catching the scent of trees and earth, of shady air. No whiff of pans—not yet. But it hardly mattered; they could not be far.

He wrinkled his nose, trotting, feeling the waves of anticipation in him rise. A sense of reckless abandon seethed in him. They were warriors, dangerous and fierce, and on their way into a skirmish. Ears pricked, nostrils wide, his eyes scanning ahead, Jan listened to the crying of herons falling away into the distance behind.

They kept at a jogtrot into the middle afternoon. The whooping voices of the herons had long since faded. Jan snorted, frowning. His anticipation waned; his limbs felt sore. Korr had trotted toward the fore of the line a half hour gone.

Now, as Tek strayed near, Jan could bear it no more.

"Hist, Tek," he whispered, and the young mare turned. "When will we come upon the pans?"

She blinked. "Never, Alma be kind, and if we go carefully."

Jan shook his head, not understanding. Dagg had come up alongside him now. "But," he started, "wasn't it because of pans that we broke camp so suddenly?"

Tek glanced at him. "Aye. But no fear, they're well behind us now."

Jan snorted, and astonishment went through him like a barb. "We've been going *away* from them?"

A smile sparked the young mare's eye. "What, did you think we'd sprung up to go seek them?" She broke into low laughter then. "By Alma's Beard, princeling. I never yet met a colt who could so *not* let trouble lie, but always must be up and hunting it."

Jan felt his ears burning. He wanted to bite something. He wanted to kick. "Trouble?" he cried. "They're only pans. . . ."

"Hark you," said Tek then, and her tone had lost its laughter suddenly, become that of a warrior to a foal. "We are not eaters of flesh like the gryphons, nor lovers of death like the wyrms. Nor do we bloody our hooves and our horns save at need."

She eyed him hard a moment more, then broke off and loped toward the head of the line. They had come to a stream. Jan kept his tongue and snatched a drink as they waded across. Fiercely cold, the water ran like ice along his ribs. He lashed furiously at the swarm of tiny waterwings that settled to sip his sweat.

His blood was burning still. Tek's mocking had made him feel like a fool. He was only grateful Korr had not overheard. How could he ever hope to become prince among the unicorns if he could not even remember the simplest rule of Law—one he had been hearing since birth? Warriors were sworn not to battle without cause. His flash of anger cooling now, Jan's whole frame drooped in despair.

As they emerged from the stream, the band slowed to a walk. Jan guessed the watercourse must have marked some boundary. The pans were a scattered people, divided and weak. They ran in little herds called tribes that fought for territory. His father's band must have crossed now into another tribe's demesne.

They walked in silence through the budding Woods. The sun, unseen, sank lower in the branch-woven sky, and the gnats subsided as the air began to cool. The shadows grew long. Jan tried to imagine a race that would make war upon its own kind, and could not. His own people were single, of the Circle. The unicorns were one.

The Woods around them had grown very still. Jan came out of his revery and lifted his head as he realized he had not heard a bird's cry in a quarter of an hour. He scented the air, and an

odor came to him, goatlike and salty. He had

smelled it only once before. Ahead, two warriors stood halted in their tracks, staring off into the trees.

"Dagg . . . ." Jan started.

But the splinter of falling wood cut him short. A dead cedar toppled groaning across their path. Its tangled roots, still clotted with earth, were stubby, as though they had been bitten through. Initiates whinnied, scattering in confusion. Something struck Jan on the shoulder.

He felt another sting against his fetlock—stones. The air was thick suddenly with flying stones. A sound like the voices of herons again filled the Woods, and pans poured from behind the trees. Some held what looked like rams' horns to their mouths, their cheeks puffed. The long, wavering cries were coming from the *horns*. Jan stared. He had never seen such a thing before.

"Don't scatter," Korr was thundering now above the commotion of horns. "Keep close—we'll soon outrun them. Follow the healer!"

Jan saw Teki rearing, his hide a flash of white and black. He whinnied sharply, then wheeled and charged the fallen cedar. Others flew to follow him. The goatlings, taken by surprise, fell back as the healer cleared the tree and was away.

Dagg bolted then, shouldering past Jan. The pans had ceased their standing volley and begun to charge. Jan rose, ready to strike at them, but Korr sprang to send him after Dagg with sharp nips and a curt command. Only then did Jan realize he and Dagg had stood staring when they should have been flying. The others were all over the tree and gone.

Jan heard a cry from Dagg, wheeled to see a goatling springing from behind a tree. She wrapped her forelimbs about Dagg's neck. He reared, writhing and thrashing, then kicked at another one rushing his flank. Jan yelled, charging, heard the prince's war cry behind him and the thunder of Korr's heels. Blue-bodied goatlings scattered for their lives.

Dagg freed himself and fled for the cedar, soaring over at a bound. Gathering his legs, Jan sprang after. Pans were standing on the other side. Some brandished pieces of pointed wood, strangely blackened and sharp as tusks. Dagg reared again, striking wildly at them. Jan cast about desperately for some sign of the band.

He could not spot them. They had vanished. The Woods stood so close and tangled here they could have been but twenty paces off and he would not have seen them. The clamor of horns deafened him. He could not think, and Korr was still behind them on the other side of the tree.

Jan slashed at a goatling that lunged at him, and suddenly caught sight of something in the gloom—a unicorn. It reared among the trees not ten paces from them, crying, "Follow!" and sprang away. Jan bit Dagg on the shoulder and shouted, "This way!"

He plunged after the other unicorn through a maze of shadows and trees, and heard the sound of Dagg's heels coming behind. Dense thickets closed about them. Jan caught only glimpses of their rescuer, could not even tell the color of the one who ran before. He had no idea who it was.

The land beneath his hooves fell suddenly away, and Jan stumbled into a gully between two hills. He realized he had lost sight of the one ahead of them then, and panic gripped him. He sprinted down the dry gravel wash. Dagg behind him was shouting something, but Jan ignored him, ignored everything, galloping harder. The others could not be far ahead.

"Jan!" Dagg behind him was crying. "Jan, stop. Stand!" All at once, his friend charged past him, veering across his path.

Jan ducked, trying to dodge, but the twisting river course was narrow. He plunged to a halt. "Dagg, we'll lose them!" he cried.

Dagg shook his head, nearly winded, blowing hard. "Wrong way," he gasped. "We've run wrong. Can't you hear them? They're behind."

Jan stopped shouldering, staring at him, then lifted his head and listened. Above the pounding of blood in his throat and the harshness of his own breathing, of Dagg's, he caught sound—far in the distance, just for a moment—of the whinny of unicorns in flight and the loonlike sounding of the horns.

"But how . . . ?" Jan wheeled, beside himself, still panting. His limbs twitched with fatigue. "I was following . . . ." The faint, far sounds were fading now into the utter stillness of the Woods.

Dagg shook his head. "Come, haste. We'll have to go back." He started past Jan.

"No. Hold," cried Jan suddenly. "We mustn't. The pans are between us and them now."

Dagg halted in midstep. They stood looking at each other. Above them, the sky was the color of rueberry stains, and the Woods all around had grown dusky, the silence deep. Jan shook his head and tried to think. His blood had quieted at last; his breathing stilled, and so, too, the sense of panic that had gripped him. He turned and climbed the sandy bank of the wash.

"We'll go west," he said. "The Plain lies that way, and it can't be far."

He glanced back over one shoulder at Dagg. His friend sidled, uncertain, gazing at the dark Woods before them with wide, nervous eyes. Jan turned at once and began shouldering his way through the undergrowth that bordered the wash, giving the other no time to reply. Dagg had to follow to keep him in sight.

"Let's be off, then," Jan told him. "The sun's low."

They came upon a glade just as the Woods grew too dim for them to make their way. Pans had been there, a great many of them, but the scent was old. Another scent lingered in the air as well—pungent, like cedar, and somehow dry. Jan had never met that odor before. He and Dagg emerged into the open. The sky above was purpling. Dagg turned to him.

"What now?"

"We wait," Jan told him. "The moon should be up soon. Once it gets high enough, it'll cast good light."

Dagg fell silent. They gazed about them. In the last moments of twilight, Jan studied the glade. Something about it struck him as strange; he could not quite get his teeth on it. Then he had it. The glade was round. The trees bordering the open space made a perfect Ring, and all the ground cover had been cleared from the interior. He and Dagg stood on brown, bare soil.

In the middle of the clearing lay a Circle of stones. A grayish powder lay in little heaps within, along with a few leafless twigs, oddly blackened. It was from these that the pungent aroma arose. Jan approached the Circle of stones. He stepped inside.

The dust felt soft beneath his heels, incredibly fine. The branches, puzzlingly brittle, crunched and compressed as he stepped on them. Dagg set one hoof inside the Ring as Jan bent to sniff the powdery gray stuff, savoring its acrid, aromatic scent. Dagg fidgeted suddenly and stepped back outside the stones.

"What's wrong?" Jan asked him.

"Don't stand there," Dagg told him. "It's hot."

Jan lifted his head and realized that his friend spoke true. The dust was warm beneath his hooves. But the heat felt good against the night air's chill. "I wonder what makes it so?"

"This is some sort of pan place," muttered Dagg. "Let's wait at the glade's edge."

Jan nodded over one shoulder toward the edge of the clearing. "You go," he murmured. "I'll keep watch."

So they waited, Jan within the Circle of stones, Dagg amid the darkness at the verge of the wood. And while the two of them kept watch, another watched them, unseen, from across the glade—one who had led them there, though they did not know it, for private ends: that the prince's son might see a thing no unicorn within the Ring had ever seen before.

The sky darkened through deep blue to black, then turned a dark silver. The moon rose, huge and brilliant, throwing black shadows through the trees. By its light, Jan saw countless pan tracks crisscrossing the soft earth of the glade—but his and Dagg's were the only hoofprints within the Circle of stones.

Just then, very faintly, Jan caught sound of something, a little run of sliding notes. He started, straining his eyes against the shadows beyond the glade. His heart had gone tight. He could make out nothing through the trees. Stepping from between the stones, he backed toward the wood's edge.

"Dagg," he breathed. "List."

Dagg lifted his head. "What is it?" he said lowly. "It isn't unicorns."

Jan and Dagg melted out of the moon's light into the Woods. Among the shadows now, Jan craned his neck; but still nothing met his gaze across the glade but moonlit trees. The notes came again then, just a snatch. They fluted through the dark.

"It's singing," murmured Jan, suddenly sure, "but no words to it. Like bird's song."

The sound grew clear now, continuous, one clear voice piping wordlessly up and down. Jan and Dagg stood perfectly still. As they listened, it was joined by another voice, and then a third. Three soft, sweet strains trilled in the stillness, drawing near.

Dagg sidled. "It's a night bird. It must be."

Jan shook his head. He felt no fear, only fascination now. "No bird," he breathed. "Hist, I want to listen. I want to know what creature sings so sweet."

Beside him, Dagg went rigid, his nostrils wide. "It's pans," he whispered, strangled. "I can smell them. Fly!"

Jan felt the muscles of his friend beside him bunch. "Stand still," he hissed, "or they'll see you."

Dagg hesitated. But Jan felt strangely, perfectly at ease. He wanted to see—he *had* to see—what would happen next, and he would not have Dagg bolting and spoiling it. The pans were coming into the glade.

They moved in a long file, a whole band of them, and made themselves into a Circle. Crouching and lounging, they faced inward. Jan saw small ones, weanlings the size of hares, and old ones, gaunt and gray-flanked among the rest, not just the slim, strong half-growns and warriors that had attacked them earlier. And then, within the Circle under the moon, three pans began to dance. Goat-footed, high-stepping, they moved and swayed.

"They dance," Jan murmured, with a little start of surprise.

Dagg shook his head. "Only the unicorns dance."

But it was so. The goatlings were dancing there, each dancer holding a flat bundle of marshreeds bound with grass. The reeds were bitten off in uneven lengths and, held to the pursed lips of the dancers, they produced the high, sweet singing.

Those watching from the Circle nodded as the dancers passed, glancing at one another, snuffling and making small gestures. Jan felt a tremor down his spine.

"They're talking to each other," he breathed.

Dagg, pressing against him, muttered doggedly, "Pans can't talk."

Jan shook his head. "With the pipes," he whispered. "With their forelimbs." A flash of insight went through him then, hot and sharp. "And they were talking to each other earlier, with their rams' horns in the Woods."

Dagg stood silent a moment, watching the glade. The dancers piped and turned. The watchers murmured, nodding. Dagg shrugged. "Not talking—they can't be. It's just chatter."

Jan shook his head again, but kept his tongue. It *was* speech, he was sure of it. Then that legend of the pans in the old lays must be false. The goatlings were *not* speechless, had not turned away the Mother's gift. The discovery astonished him. He strained his ears to the pipes, his eyes to the intricate movements of those strangely jointed forelimbs, and felt the uncanny certainty that if only he could watch long enough, listen deeply enough, he could come to understand.

Dagg beside him shifted suddenly. "What's happening?"

Jan came back to himself. He realized the snuffling murmur was dying now. A hush followed. One by one the dancers handed their pipes to members of the Ring, and for three moments in turn one strain of the music paused, and then resumed.

The dancers caught up blackened stakes, the male brandishing one in each forelimb like long, straight hooves. Each female held one stake to her forehead like a horn. They snorted, tossing their heads, and pawed at the earth. Jan felt a rush of recognition.

"It's a singer's tale," he hissed. "They're telling it—but without words."

The two females circled lazily within the goatlings' Ring, seemingly unaware of the male stalking them. The music of the flutes grew soft and secretive. Suddenly, the male caught up a branch and threw it down before his quarry. The females whirled, leaping back as if surprised as the other sprang up, brandishing his stakes. The panpipes shrilled.

The mock unicorns lowered their heads and charged, the pointed stakes at their foreheads aimed—but the male batted them lightly away. Once more the females charged and again were put to flight. This time the male pursued them, round the inside of the Ring, until his quarry at last outdistanced him.

The male pan halted, raising his forelimbs, his head thrown back in triumph. The fluting of the panpipes swelled. The mock unicorns straggled away in defeat. The dancers left the inside of the Ring, rejoining their fellows at the rim.

"The ambuscade," murmured Jan. He was shaking, but from astonishment, not fear. "They were telling the others how they put us to flight."

"But," Dagg hissed through clamped teeth, "that isn't how it happened at all!" The interior of the pans' Ring lay empty now. The fluting continued, very soft. "They didn't rout us," Dagg insisted. "We didn't *deign* to fight. . . ."

He had no time to finish, for Jan beside him had caught in his breath.

"Oh," the prince-son breathed, brushing his shoulder against his companion to still him. "Oh, Dagg. What's that?"

A pan had risen from the Ring and now was kneeling beside the Circle of stones. With a sheaf of reeds, she brushed aside the gray powder. A second pan came to the stones and threw down a heap of dead branches. Small lights, like red stars, leapt upward through the twigs.

Then something flickered upon the branches, something bright. Jan stared, overtaken with wonder. The stuff upon the twigs—it moved, it danced. It was the color of his mother's coat, of a setting sun. It flowed like a unicorn's mane, like grass in the wind, like . . . like . . . . He could not say. The branches beneath it blackened and curled. And some began to glow, orange red, then broke at last and fell into a fine, gray dust.

It cast a fleeting light upon the bodies of the pans. They crowded closer, holding their forelimbs to it. Jan saw their bluish hides trickling sweat, even in the chill night air. Mist rose from the flaring stuff, tendrils that to Jan seemed black against the hoary moon, and pale against the sky.

"Prince-son," a voice behind him breathed, "and Dagg. Stand still and do not speak. It is I."

Jan started and wheeled, then felt sudden relief flooding through him as he recognized the healer's daughter. She had slipped up between them in the dark.

"Come away, softly now," she said. "I'll take you to the others. They are not far."

Dagg turned hurriedly to follow her. Jan heard him sighing with relief. But the prince's son had to force himself to go. He wanted to stand watching forever under the moon and the stars. He fell in slowly behind Dagg and the healer's daughter. They skirted the glade. Then without a backward glance, Tek struck out into the dark. Jan sighed, following her. He caught a last glimpse of the pans in their Ring through the trees. A handful of them had begun once more to dance.

"They danced," said Jan, after a time.

Tek looked at him. "The pans? I saw none dancing, young prince."

"Before you came," he answered, "and just now, as we left. They were beautiful."

He stopped short, saying it—for only now as he spoke did he realize that it was so. There had been a strange grace in those upright, two-footed forms, a litheness in those odd forelimbs unlike any grace a unicorn could ever have. Jan saw Dagg eyeing him over the back of the healer's daughter.

"Pans?" he cried. "Those twisted little haunts crept up and fell on us this day, without cause."

"We're in their land without their leave," answered Jan, but so softly he was speaking to himself. That thought, too, was new—it had just come to him. Dagg paid no heed. Jan saw him screwing shut his eyes.

"They're like hillcats. They clutched our manes and tried to pull us down. . . ." Jan saw him shudder.

"Peace," murmured Tek.

Jan turned to her. "Was it you," he asked her, "who led us off? You've been ahead of us all this time?"

The young mare looked at him. "Led you off? I only came upon you a few moments gone, out scouting for stragglers."

"There was another then," Jan told her. "I heard . . . I saw . . . ."

The healer's daughter laughed, but gently. "Thought you heard or saw, perhaps? Come, it's easy to imagine haunts and followers in a dark wood at night."

Jan shook his head; he had not meant that at all—but they had reached the others now. Jan spotted them through the trees ahead, in a glade almost at the wood's edge. He saw the moon shining white upon the Plain not twenty paces farther on. Korr stood with Teki across the open space. The prince shifted impatiently, staring back toward the Woods. He seemed to be attending to the healer's words with only half an ear.

Jan followed Tek and Dagg past the sentries into the glade. Spotting them, the prince broke off from Teki and came forward. Those not standing guard had already lain down among the bracken. Korr nodded Dagg away to join the others. Jan halted and gazed at the dark figure standing before him.

"Struck off to delve the Pan Woods on your own?" the prince said curtly. He stood against the moon, a black shadow against its light. Jan could not see his face. "Did you not hear my order to keep together?"

His father's rebuke felt like the slash of hooves. Jan flinched. "We lost sight of the others," he started.

"Dawdling when I told you to fly."

Jan dropped his head. "We ran wrong," he mumbled, picking at the turf with one forehoof. "But we knew if we went westward we'd reach the Plain."

He heard his father sigh. "Well, I suppose that was clever enough," he conceded at last. "If only you were half so clever at staying clear of trouble as you seem to be at finding it." He snorted again. "Heed what I tell you in future," he added. "And stay with the band. Now find you forage, and rest. The Plain is harder going than the Woods."

Korr turned away then, lashing his tail, though there were no flies now, only night millers and moths. Jan gazed after the prince as he went to stand staring out over the moonlit Plain. His heart felt hollow, filled with an ache too keen to bear. He had lost his father's praise.

"You are a silent one for thought," Tek said to him. With a start, he realized the healer's daughter had not left his side. He said the first thing that came into his head.

"I . . . was thinking of the pans." And saying so, he did think of them. The memory of their beauty eased his heart a little. He turned to her. Her eyes were clear, green stones lit by moonlight. "Was it fire?"

She shook her head, clearly puzzled. "A huddle of pans under the moon was all I saw."

"But . . . ," he started. Then he felt sleep catching at his mane and had to swallow a yawn.

"Enough," the young mare said. "The moon's halfway up into the sky. Time enough for talk tomorrow, on the Plain. Good rest."

She bowed to him, going to seek her place among the sentries. Jan bowed in return and, finding where Dagg had lain, he lay down beside him. His limbs felt loose and empty with fatigue. His thoughts were growing woolly, slow. Even the sting of his father's ire was numbing. Nothing seemed to matter now but sleep.

He closed his eyes, images flaring before his inner gaze like flame. By morning, he could not recall, but that night he dreamed of goatlings dancing under the bright egg of the moon.

THE PLAIN

When Alma made the world, she made the heart of the world first, which was fire, and then the air above the world, and then the sea that girdles the world, and lastly the land. Woods, mountains, and valleys she made, each where each was fitting. But most of the land she shaped into the Plain—not level, but rolling, a vast expanse of gentle rises and wrinkles and rolls.

Korr kept them moving all day their first day upon Alma's back, loping in long easy strides where the ground was smooth or downsloping, checking to a trot where it steepened or grew rough. The moon, huge and yellow, floated beside them on the horizon's edge in the hour after dawn before it set.

They lay up at noon for an hour's rest in a shallow hollow between two rills. Jan threw himself down beside Dagg, panting. His muscles ached and trembled as they cooled. Then before he had even half caught his breath it seemed, they were off again.

Just before dusk, Korr brought them to a halt. Jan's legs folded under him, his eyelids sliding shut of their own accord. He was asleep before he knew. Later, Dagg roused him, and in the dark after sundown they tasted their first grass since they had left the Vale—tender, green, and marvelously sweet.

The land remained hilly as they moved northward. The Pan Woods and the Gryphon Mountains beyond dwindled in the distance, becoming a dark line on the horizon behind them, then vanished at last. Jan felt his muscles hardening, his flanks growing leaner and his stride rangier as each day rolled on.

It was their third morning out of the Woods. The dew was still thick upon the grass, the sun in the east barely risen over the flat rim of the world. Jan's limbs, still stiff from sleep, were beginning to limber. The band had not yet broken camp.

"Well," Jan was saying as his long, slim horn clattered against Dagg's, "what do you think?"

Dagg parried him.

"Keep your guard up," he heard Tek saying.

Jan countered Dagg's sudden thrust and threw him off. They reared together, shoulder-wrestling for a moment.

"Think of what?" Dagg asked him, struggling.

"About the Firebringer," Jan panted, shifting his weight. "That he'll be the color-of-night, and a great warrior. . . ."

He braced himself and Dagg slipped from him. The two of them rolled, then scrabbled to their feet and fenced a little, tentatively.

"More force, Jan," he heard Tek telling him. "You foot as though this were a dance."

But it was, in a way, he thought as Dagg and he dodged, paused, parried, measured, each advancing and giving ground by turns. But he kept his tongue. Dagg was lunging at him.

"The Firebringer? But that's history. Zod the singer saw him."

Jan fended his friend's slow, hard jabs with a half-dozen light taps.

"More force!" called Tek.

Jan parried harder. "But only in a dream."

"A seer's dream."

"List, *faster,* Dagg," the young mare instructed. Jan glimpsed her sidling for a better view. Dagg pivoted, grazing him. The sudden sting surprised him. Jan knocked his friend's horn away.

"I know," he breathed, throwing himself after Dagg. "But do seers' dreams always come to pass?" Taking advantage of his friend's misstep, Jan rained a volly of feints and thrusts. Dagg was too hard pressed to answer. "Tek?" panted Jan. "Does it?"

"Well enough, let be," he heard the healer's daughter laughing. "Enough hornplay for now. We've a day's running ahead of us yet."

Jan and Dagg fell apart, catching their breath. As Tek turned away, they followed her to the edge of the loose Ring of resting unicorns, away from the clash of other pilgrims, early risen, still learning battlecraft. The healer's daughter turned to Jan.

"Until he come, little prince," she said, "all we may know of the Firebringer is what Zod and other dreamers said of him: that he shall come on hooves so hard and sharp they will strike sparks upon the stone. That his blood shall be of burning, and his tongue a flit of flame. That he may not come until the Circle has been broken. And his birth shall mark both the beginning and the ending of an age."

Jan shook his head, frowning at her words. Dawn wind was rising now. "I thought only Zod had foretold the Firebringer."

The healer's daughter shook her shoulders. "Others have seen him. Caroc foretold he would be born out of a wyvern's belly, and Ellioc that he would not come from within the Ring at all, but outside it—a Renegade. . . ."

"But Caroc and Ellioc were false prophetesses," Dagg said impatiently. "Nothing either of them foretold has ever come to pass. . . ."

"Yet," murmured Tek. Dagg snorted.

"How could a unicorn be born out of a wyvern's belly?" He swatted a blackfly from his haunch. "The only one who ever truly saw the Firebringer was Zod."

Tek stood three-legged, cocking her head to scratch her cheek with one heel. "Oh, truly?" she murmured. "Then I suppose I have not seen him."

Jan looked at her. "You saw . . ." he began. "Where, when?"

The young mare straightened, shaking herself. "Not in flesh. In a dream."

Dagg came forward. "Is *that* why you changed the ending of the lay, the one you sang at Moondance?"

Tek glanced at him, and let go a nickering laugh. "So far, you seem to be the only one to have remarked it." She laughed again, half at herself. "Perhaps the others were all already asleep."

"The Beard," Jan heard Dagg breathe. "I told you she was a dreamer."

The young mare sighed. "No dreamer. Only a little of a singer, and a warrior. I saw the Firebringer on the night all unicorns are dreamers: at my initiation, two years gone."

Jan snorted. "What do you mean?"

Tek looked at him. "You have not heard? I thought all colts found out before the time, though they are not meant to."

Jan studied her, and she was laughing at him with her green, green eyes—taunting him, daring him. But he refused to be baited. He only said, softly, "Will you tell us of it, of initiation?"

She nodded then, shrugging. "I suppose. You'll find out soon enough in any case." And she made her voice low, like a singer's cant. Both colts had to lean closer to hear. "Those who have come far over Alma's back, kept Ring and borne themselves bravely—those whom the Mother finds worthy—will at dawn behold a true vision of their destinies upon the Mirror of the Moon."

Jan's heart missed a step. "Their destinies," he

whispered, gazing at Tek. She sighed, her eyes fixed, unfocused now.

"Only a glimpse. A glimpse."

"And you saw the Firebringer."

She had turned a little away from him. "I saw the moon crack like a bird's egg and fall out of the sky, and from the broken shell stepped forth a young unicorn, long limbed and lithe, a runner, a dancer, and black as the well of a weasel's eye. He looked exactly as the old song says:

"The silver moon rode on his brow,
And a white star on his heel."

"But," said Jan; he had to force himself to speak slowly, "if you saw him born . . . ." Excitement flared in him. "Then that can only mean the Firebringer will come among us in your lifetime."

Tek glanced at Jan, then Dagg. She laughed, casting a glance at Korr. "Perhaps. Or perhaps he is already among us, only waiting to be known."

Jan turned to gaze after his father, who stood a little apart from the band, watching the fiery dish of the sun pull free of the horizon. Korr was a mighty prince, a fleet runner, a fine dancer. And he was black, black as a starless night. Did Tek think Korr might be the one—did others think it? Dagg had hinted as much at Moondance, days ago.

Jan felt a rush of longing then. Was there nothing he could do to win back his father's esteem? And though the prince had not a mark of white or silver on him, odd spots, appearing suddenly, were not unknown among the unicorns. One never knew what lay beneath until spring shed.

Tek started away from him, murmuring, "We'll be breaking camp soon."

Jan let go his daydreaming and yawned, shaking himself. Dagg shouldered against him. The grass before them billowed and stirred. As Dagg lowered his head to nibble the tender green shoots, Jan turned to follow Tek. There had been something more he had wanted to ask her. The sun was up, the waning moon in the western sky well past its zenith. Tek was rousing those who were dozing still.

"Hist, Tek," said Jan lowly. The healer's daughter turned. "Where were you off to, night past?"

The young mare frowned and shook her head. "I stood sentry before dawn, if that's what you mean."

She turned and woke another pilgrim. Jan waited till they were out of others' earshot again. "Earlier—before moonrise."

Tek halted and studied him keenly. "Breaking the Ring is forbidden," she told him. "And straying away would be madness at night. There are grass pards on this Plain."

Jan shook his head. "I saw you."

Teki had sung them a lay after dusk, how Alma created her own being from a dance of light in the Great Darkness before time, and the world was but a droplet shaken from her as a young mare shakes bright water from her coat. Afterward, as the others around him had drifted into sleep, Jan had lain restless, gazing off into the dark.

The sentries, at last getting their turn to eat, had torn at the young grass too greedily to keep good watch. Then Jan had caught a hint of motion from the corner of his eye and turned to see a unicorn slipping away from camp, half hidden by the folds and rills of land, then striking out at a fast, silent lope in the direction whence they had come.

He stood gazing at Tek as she eyed him now in the light of broken day. "I have gone nowhere, young princeling," she answered, suddenly formal, then turned to rouse another initiate. "You must have dreamed it."

Jan watched her go. It had been no dream. Tek's own mother, Jah-lila, had banished his dreams when he was small. Surely the pied mare could not have forgotten that. He had not been able to see the other's color, night past, by the dim starlight, but the form and the gait had reminded him strongly of Tek.

She moved away from Jan, stepping among the Circle of pilgrims, murmuring for them to rise. Jan gazed after her, feeling oddly unsettled and at a loss. Sleepily, the last of the initiates rose and stretched. Korr's whistle to the band a moment later cut across Jan's thoughts, and they were off once more across the Plain.

Jan and Dagg ran with Tek, as had become their custom. Other initiates had singled out warriors to be their mentors as well. Jan said nothing more of having seen Tek slip away, and the morning drifted on. As the unicorns loped over the rolling grassland, the sun pulled higher. White clouds began to stray across the wide, blue sky.

After a time, he came aware that Dagg had drifted from them, and now was running a little apart from the band, his gaze fixed intently away. Jan followed his stare, fixing his own eyes on the far horizon and the miles of openness between. *What lay beyond there?* he wondered, the question stirring and murmuring in the back of his mind. *What lay beyond?*

Jan came back to himself with a start, as Dagg before him suddenly stumbled, missing his stride. They both had drifted even farther from the herd. How long had he been running, lost in thought? Jan wondered. The sun seemed higher. Before him Dagg snorted and tossed his head. Jan drew alongside.

"What is it?"

"Look there."

Jan scanned to westward, straining his eyes. Then he saw, suddenly, two figures very far away upon the crest of a roll. They stood splay-legged, heads high as if surprised, watching the herd loping by. They were unicorns.

"Tek!" cried Jan, veering back with Dagg toward their mentor. "Do you see them? What are they?"

He saw the healer's daugher turn and her green eyes narrow as she spotted the figures on the distant rise. She glanced at Jan. "Renegades."

Jan wrenched his gaze back to the pair. They had passed the midpoint of his gaze, and he had to turn to keep them in view. Renegades—those who had deserted the Vale, forsaken Alma and broken the Ring of Law. Outcasts, criminals, infidels. *And I almost became one of them,* he found himself thinking, his mind going back to the day of the gryphons. Jan stared at the figures on the hill.

"Watch," Tek was telling him.

She let loose a long, loud warrior's cry. The pair upon the hillside started and wheeled, vanishing over the crest of the rise. Jan thought he could hear their wild, high whinnies very faintly on the breeze. He saw his father snorting, refusing to acknowledge the Ringbreakers' presence by so much as a glance. The band galloped on.

Time passed. Hours, and then days, almost a dozen of them. Sunrises and moonsets fell behind them as they ran, and the land seemed to roll away under their hooves. For Jan, their days were all loping, snatched rest, and sparring. The warriors taught them battlecraft, how to stalk, how to follow a trail. The healer told them the properties of herbs and where to find water on the Great Grass Plain.

Their nights were all greedy feeding and singers' tales and sleep. Korr showed them how to find their way using the stars. The whole sky had become strangely tilted now; new starshapes looming before them as they traveled north, the old ones slipping beyond the world's rim behind.

Sometimes at night now, gazing into the pattern of Alma's eyes, Jan felt himself taken from himself, made hollow. If only he gazed long enough, deeply enough, it seemed he might begin to read some great mystery in their turning, something deeper than simply where on the world he stood. As if the stars might, very gently, bear him away.

But despite the unceasing cycle of busyness and rest, busyness and rest, Jan felt a restlessness within him growing. Though he guarded himself very close now, keeping himself always within the band as his father had commanded, more and more he found himself gazing off across the Plain. That strange little voice he could not quite hear whispered in his mind still: *What lies beyond your band, beyond the vastness of the Plain? Come, come away. Come see.*

Sometimes, in the distance behind, he glimpsed a figure that did not stop and stare at them, as Renegades did. And sometimes he caught the far, faint drum of heels after the band had already come to a halt. Only Tek seemed restless, too, though she said no word. Twice more he glimpsed her slipping off into the dark.

Something moved out there, just beyond his range. He felt it to the marrow of his bones. Not all its cunning could keep him from beginning to suspect that something watched him, or awaited him, or both. Its hold on him that had blocked his vision for so long, at last was growing tenuous.

So it kept itself nearby, but circumspect. And the prince's son stayed baffled still, for it dared not risk letting him—letting any of them—learn who it was that ran behind.

The twelfth day of their travel upon the Mare's back was stretching on toward noon. Jan and Dagg ran with Tek near the middle of the band. A light rain must have fallen the night before, for the ground over which they ran was damp. They had seen no hard rains yet upon the Plain.

The prince before them crested a rise, and Jan saw his father come suddenly to a standstill. At his whistle, the pilgrims plunged to a halt. Jan stood a moment, puzzled; the day was early yet for halting. The sun had not yet topped the sky.

Jan trotted forward, and a few others followed. He halted near his father, who stood gazing down the slope. Then Jan started and cavaled as he saw what had caught the prince's eye. Below them lay a unicorn, pale blue and bloodied, her horn stained red. The great vein of her throat had been torn; talons had scored her flank and neck. Nearby lay a banded pard, gored through one shoulder and the ribs of one battered side staved in from a mighty kick.

No spotted kites yet circled the sky. The blood upon the grass was wet. Jan stared, realizing: It could not have happened an hour gone. He heard his father give a great snort, then, as though he had unwittingly smelled fetor.

"Pard," Korr muttered, starting downslope at an angle, away from the dead. "Renegade."

"See the mistake she made," Jan heard Tek telling Dagg. "She let it clasp her by the throat." Her warrior's voice was flat, dispassionate. Jan wheeled to stare. "If ever one of those springs on you, buck—roll. Don't gore. Use your heels—and run."

Jan turned back to the fallen mare, pity mingling with his horror. She was so young; she could not have been much older than Tek. And she had died bravely, fighting for her life—*as I once fought for my life,* Jan found himself thinking, *not so long ago.*

Others of the band, he realized, were already following the prince. Though some of the initiates still stood staring, the warriors turned them, hurrying them off, themselves trotting by the dead with hardly a glance.

"But," Jan started, "shouldn't we bury her?"

The prince broke into a lope at the bottom of the hill, whistling the others to follow him.

"But," cried Jan, "she's dead. Shouldn't there be rites?"

His father wheeled. "Less noise," he called. "We move on."

Jan stared in disbelief. They could not simply abandon the dead. It was against Alma's Law. It was shameful. "We can't go yet," he burst out. "A warrior deserves . . . ."

At that, Korr wheeled and smote the ground with his forehooves. "Hold your tongue," he thundered. "*That* is no warrior." He tossed his head toward the fallen mare. "She was a Renegade, and died as all outside the Circle must—unmarked and unmourned. The Law is not for her. Now come."

Others of the band had strayed to a stop, stood watching the prince of the unicorns and his son. Korr wheeled away. Jan stood confounded. A Renegade? But she bore a horn upon her brow. Her hooves were cloven still, not solid round and single-toed. And even if she were a Renegade, what could that matter now? She was a unicorn, and she was dead.

His father gave no backward glance. Jan found himself shouting, "This isn't right!"

But a sharp nip on the flank cut him short. He spun around. Tek shouldered against him, shoving him after the herd.

"Enough," she whispered. "Don't contest with your father."

"No, it's wrong," cried Jan, "leaving her." He threw his weight back, resisting. He felt hot and rash.

Tek bullied him forward, nearly knocking him down.

 "Be still, Jan. Just come!" he heard Dagg call.

The prince and the others were cantering away. Dagg lingered, but Teki shouldered against him, turning him. Dagg tried to duck around, dodge back to Jan, but the healer herded him away after the rest. Dagg gazed back over his shoulder helplessly. Jan stared. The others' dust clouded the air. Another sharp nip on the flank brought him back to himself.

"Hie!" Tek shouted. "*Now,* or we'll not catch them till noon."

Jan kicked into a gallop, seething with rage. He and Tek breathed dust, running hard for a mile until they caught the herd. Korr called a halt not long after. Jan threw himself down at the edge of the Ring. At the prince's nod, Teki kept Dagg with him across the Ring, away from Jan. The healer began to sing them a lay.

"I'll tell you now of the Renegades, how each was a unicorn once, but failed initiation, or else was banished for murder or some other crime, or else faithlessly broke Ring and ran away to live wild, godless, Lawless, hated of Alma upon the Plain. . . ."

Jan could not listen. His thoughts were in a snarl. Fury made his jaw ache, his ears burn. His blood felt feverish. After a moment, he pitched to his feet and left the Ring. Tek beside him showed no interest at his going. The others were all either absorbed in the tale or intentionally ignoring him, as Korr was. Jan trotted around a low rise, out of sight of the camp. He had to get away.

The sentry eyed him indifferently, then turned

his attention back to the camp. Jan pawed the turf, frustration biting at him. He did not care if the mare *had* been a Renegade. What they had done was dishonorable, simply leaving her, as if she had been no more than a dead gryphon or pan. No! Jan shook his head. She was a unicorn. She had killed a pard at the cost of her life and deserved a hero's death rites.

Something occurred to him then, a possibility he had not considered before. He halted, turning it over in his mind. Did he really need anybody's leave? Anyone might perform the rites. And if he ran quick and light, keeping low behind the brow of the swells before striking out across the Plain, he could be halfway back to the mare before he was spotted—if he was spotted. It was almost like a game.

Jan glanced at the sentry on the hill. The warrior's ears were still pricked to the sound of Teki's voice, his gaze inward turned, not scanning the Plain as it should have been. Jan made up his mind in a rush and plunged into the dry gully across from him, putting another rise between himself and the camp.

He followed the streambed back the way they had come, then clambered up the short, steep bank onto the grass again. Behind him, the sentry was a small, gray figure against the sky, and the fallen Renegade lay only a couple of miles' hard gallop off. Jan sprinted across the Plain.

 The Renegade was not difficult to find. Spotted

kites had begun to circle now. At home, in the Vale, Jan had seen the rites for the dead, how the fallen were laid upon the outer cliffs with forelegs extended, their heads thrown back, manes streaming and their hind legs kicked out behind. Nearing the spot where the dark birds circled, he told himself he would lay out the fallen mare and be back to noon camp before he could be missed.

Jan topped the gentle rise before the slope on which the Renegade and the pard that had felled her lay—then pitched to a halt, snorting, staring. Someone had been there before him, and whoever it was had been laying out the grasscat as well. The pard lay stretched now, paws folded, a Circle trampled in the grass all around—just as for a warrior.

Jan glanced about him, puzzled, and suddenly uneasy, wondering whom he had interrupted at the rites. He gave a whinny, then another, and listened. No answer came. The legs of the mare had been laid, but her head was not yet lifted. The Circle about her was only half complete. The shadows of the dark birds wheeled and floated over the grass.

He had no time to waste on wondering. Jan descended the slope. He took the young mare's horn in his teeth—carefully, lest it prove brittle. To his surprise, it was strong and hard. Horn in teeth, he lifted her head and laid it so her silvery mane streamed long and knotted on the grass. He had to work quickly. The kites were dropping lower in the sky.

He had just finished the stamping of the Circle about her when he caught the sound of hoofbeats. He whirled, fearing for a moment that it was members of his own band, before realizing that the sound came from the wrong quarter, from the west.

A unicorn topped the rise. He was young, no older than Dagg's young mother, Leerah, and color-of-evening-sky. His mane was long, with feathers tangled in it. He bore a horn upon his brow. A pale orange mare joined him in a moment, then a crimson filly almost half-grown. They stared at Jan. Jan stared at them. They all had horns. The evening blue came a few steps down the slope.

"What do you here?" His words were quiet, odd. A moment passed before Jan understood him.

"I was burying them," he answered. "Weren't you here before?"

The other shook his head.

"We saw the kites," the pale mare said.

The blue was eyeing him more closely now. "You have not the look of one from the Plain," he said. "Nor the speech of one, either. Whence come you?"

Jan gazed at them, startled. "I come from the Vale of the Unicorns. On Pilgrimage."

All three of the strangers started.

"He's a Moondancer," the pale mare muttered. "One of those who drink of the wyvern pool."

Jan glanced at the dead mare, then turned to the one who stood before him. "I didn't start to bury her," he said. "I only finished the rite. Was it none of you?"

The dark blue unicorn shook his head. "Nay. And I know of no one else who runs in these parts this moon. It must have been the Far One."

"The Fair One," the pale mare said, and the filly echoed, "The Red One, the Rare One."

"She is often on the Plain in spring," the blue unicorn added, and Jan realized he must have looked confounded. "She is a strange, dark mallow color, without any yellow or amber in it. She is holy, and very wise. Her hooves are oddly made, for she comes from a far place. And once, it is said, she was not a unicorn."

Jan had to listen very hard to be able to follow. Their speech was strange, like a singer's cant—and much of it he did not understand at all.

"She is known and welcomed everywhere among the Free People," the crimson filly said.

Jan shook his head; he had never heard of such a one. "You have seen her?" he asked.

Now the filly shook her head.

"They say a young prince of the southlands found her, years ago, lost and wandering," the orange mare said. She came a few steps downslope to stand beside the blue. "He told her of the wyvern country far across the Plain, that she might go there in summer, and drink of a miraculous spring that would make her a unicorn."

"What prince was that?" cried Jan. He had never heard of such a deed in song or lay.

"The one whose name means 'thunder,' " the blue one said. "The black one . . . ." He glanced at the mare beside him.

She told him, "Korr."

Jan started like a deer. "My fa . . . ." He caught himself. "A prince of the unicorns would never do such a thing—let drink of the scared pool one who was not of the Circle."

"Circle?" the red filly asked.

Jan stared at them. "Don't you know? You're Renegades."

"Renegades," the evening blue murmured, tasting the word as though it were strange upon his tongue.

"Weren't you born of the Circle, in the Vale of the Unicorns?"

The blue shook his head. "I was born here, on the Plain."

Jan breathed out hard, feeling as if his ribs had been kicked. They were not of the Circle, had never been of the Circle. They were not runaways from his people at all. They were, instead, of another clan, another—he searched for the word—*tribe* altogether, like the gryphons, like the pans.

Then his skin grew cold. For they were unicorns. They had never sipped of the Mirror of the Moon, yet their horns had not fallen, nor their cloven hooves grown single and round. Wispy tassels tipped their ears, and their heels were fringed with silky hair. They were bearded. He could not seem to catch his breath.

The blue unicorn shrugged. "I have always lived here."

"*I* have heard of this Circle of the southerners," the pale mare said, coming forward now again, "this Ring of War, this Circle of the Moon—and your Vale. My mother fled them when she was no more than a filly." Her words were sharp. "She said you southlanders think much of your Ring, and bind yourselves to it until you cannot see or say or think or do a thing that is not within it."

She tossed her head and snorted.

"Well, we are not bound to your Circle. We come and think and say as we please. We are the Free People."

Jan blinked and stared at her. He had never been so spoken to in all his life. And what was this they said of Korr—that he had broken the Circle, broken the Law, to tell the secret way to the Mirror of the Moon to one who was not even a unicorn. Or what had they said? Who had *once* not been a unicorn? He saw the blue unicorn eyeing the sky. The shadows of the kites had grown sharper, their spirals tighter. They circled lower to the ground.

"The time turns short that it would be proper to remain here," the blue unicorn said. "Soon it will be the kites' time."

Jan's gaze went once more to the fallen mare, pale middle blue against the dark earth of the Plain. Her blood on the grass was dry. She looked as though she were springing free of the Ring that encircled her. He glanced at the dark blue unicorn with feathers in his hair.

"Did you know her?" Jan asked him. The other shook his head. Jan turned back to the fallen one. "We have a song for the dead," he said, "when we lay them out to greet the sky:

"Fate has unspoken one of the Circle,
Pride of companions, wonted of fame.
Vouch for her valor, her heart of a hero,
Fellow of warriors, fallen in battle:
Rally, remember her name."

He was no singer, but his voice was young and strong. Jan stopped himself at the last word.

"I don't know her name," he said.

"The Mother knows," said the blue unicorn beside him.

The filly told him, "Álm'harat knows."

Jan turned, drawn up short again with wonder—though he was already so stunned it almost seemed nothing should surprise him anymore—that any dared speak the truename of Alma here, so openly. He had always been taught that those outside the Ring had cast off the Mother-of-all, had forgotten her.

The plainsdwellers joined him at the Circle's edge. He saw them dip their heads, going down on one knee first to the fallen mare, then to the pard. Jan blinked, frowning. It was no gesture he had ever seen before. He bowed his own head to the mare, then after a pause, to the grasscat as well. The plainsdwellers rose.

Then the pale orange mare turned to him and went down again on one knee for a moment before him. Jan drew back, not knowing what to make of it.

"My words were harsh to you before, young stranger," she said, rising. "For that, I ask your pardon. You have honored our dead in accordance with your custom, and that is unlike any southlander I have ever heard of."

"And you have honored her slain enemy as well, as is fitting," the blue unicorn said. "That, too, is unlike what we have heard of southlanders."

"I didn't," Jan started. "We don't . . . ." He stopped and gazed at the three plainsdwellers before him. Then he blurted out, "A gryphon came, a month ago. . . ."

"Gryphon?" the red filly said.

"It's like a pard," cried Jan, "but wingèd." He caught himself. Why was it so urgent he give these strangers only the truth?

" 'Wingcats,' my mother called them," the pale mare murmured. "They don't come here."

Jan drew breath and made his voice as steady as he could. "We killed it—it had attacked us—but we didn't bury it. We cast it over the cliff."

The dark blue unicorn frowned. "That is strange."

"Why do you dishonor your enemies?" the red filly asked. "Was this wingcat not brave?"

"Is all that is true to its own nature not worthy of honor," the evening blue said, "being part of the Cycle?"

A kite passed very close overhead. Jan felt the wind of its passing against his brow. He flinched, frowning. "I thought you said you disdained our Circle. . . ."

The plainsdweller shook his head. "Nay. That is not the Cycle of which I spoke . . . hist. Come away."

A kite had alighted on the grass, across the Circle from them. Jan came with them, following the plainsdwellers up the slope. The sky in the south was dark with cloud. More kites were settling on the grass below. The blue unicorn raised his head, his nostrils wide.

"A storm's in the wind," he said.

Jan glanced at the sun. "I have to go back," he told them. "Noon's almost done."

"Farewell, then, young stranger," the evening blue said.

"Swift running," said the pale mare, "and no pards behind you."

"Light sleeping," the filly bade him. "Far seeing."

"Alma keep you," Jan found himself saying. He was bowing—he almost wished he could stay. They were so strange—unicorns, yet not like his own people at all. He wished he could understand them, grasp more of what they had said to him, but he dared not linger. The band would be breaking camp before long. He could not stay.

The plainsdwellers dipped to their knees in leave-taking, then wheeled, whinnying and tossing their heads, and galloped off across the Plain to the west. Jan shook himself, then turned at last. The storm in the south had drawn nearer. He sprinted northward. Behind him, the spotted kites were dropping from the sky.

He found the gully he had followed before and slipped into its shelter long before the gray speck of a sentry could take note of him. He sprinted along the dry channel's flat, even bed until he was almost to camp. The lookout on the hill above was still attending to Teki's lay. Jan crept past, around the rise. The unicorns yet rested in their Ring, all eyes upon the healer reciting his tale:

"So that is the lay of Aras, the first Renegade, false Ringbreaker, who spurned Halla the princess's rule and forsook the herd. . . ."

Jan spotted Dagg across the Ring, staring off miserably at nothing. Korr's gaze was turned pointedly away from Jan's empty spot. As Jan slipped into place beside the healer's daughter, Tek hardly glanced at him. Teki was singing:

"So he perished horribly, as I have told, for Alma's wrath. And all of this took place after the unicorns had been cast out of the Hallow Hills, but before they came upon the Vale that is now our home. My tale is done."

Jan lay at the Ring's edge, catching his breath. No one even seemed to have noticed he had been gone.

Teki finished his tale, and the unicorns broke camp. They trotted at first to loosen their limbs. Jan felt wobbly, short of breath—he had spent none of the noon halt resting—and Korr still kept Dagg between him and the healer, apart from Jan. A line of tall, dark thunderheads crowded the distance behind.

By midafternoon they had swallowed the sun, bringing in their shadow a rush of cool, southern air. Jan felt his old wildness at thunderstorms rising. Stormwind riffled his winter coat, lifting the dust, bowing the grass. The smell of water hung in the wind. Then the gusts grew stronger suddenly, buffeting, the dust rising in whirlwinds.

Korr whistled the band to a faster lope, and Jan wondered if he hoped to outrun the storm. If so, it was to no avail, for within minutes rain began to lash at them. The stormshadow around them had grown very dark. Great bolts of blue lightning vaulted overhead.

And then Jan caught sound of something, another sound above the rain. It was a rushing as of many gryphons' wings, a roar like hillsides breaking and plunging away. One moment it sounded faint and far, the next almost upon them, coming and going in the gusts of storm. Ahead of him, Jan saw his father's head come up.

"Gallop!" thundered the prince. "Full gallop, all!"

The band sprang into a run.

"What is it?" cried Jan, drawing alongside Tek.

"Serpent-cloud," she shouted at him. "A great destroyer!"

Jan felt his legs tangle, his breath grow short. The old lays sang of Serpent-clouds, great tunnels of storm that ran down Ringbreakers and Renegades. He cast a wild glance over one shoulder, but could see nothing for the blinding, choking rain.

"Where is it?" he shouted at Tek. "How if it catches us?"

"Fling us to bits," the young mare answered. "So fly!"

They ran. The ground over which they galloped was slick, treacherous with mud. Thunder snorted and stamped. Jan felt the herd around him growing ragged. The eyes of some had begun to roll. Lightning fell to the right and left of them, the band flinching and veering at every crash.

"Shelter!" he heard someone to the fore of them crying. "Shelter ahead!"

Jan felt the pitch of the ground rise under his

feet, then curve and fall abruptly away. He vaulted into a gully and then flung himself backward, folding his legs. Tek was scrambling into place beside him. They lay, shouldered into the steep curve of the bank, sheltered somewhat from the driving rain. But above the fury of thunder and wind, he still heard the wild crooning of the Serpent-cloud.

"Where's Dagg?" Jan said suddenly, and flung a glance over his shoulder. "Dagg?"

He searched the downpour, up and down the line of other unicorns crowding the gully. He did not see him. Where was he—had he fallen? Was he still out upon the Plain? Jan bolted to his feet and struggled up over the bank again, shouting his friend's name. Tek scrambled after him.

"What is it?" she cried. "What are you doing?"

The stormrain whipped at his face, his eyes. "It's Dagg!" he flung back. "I don't see him. Da . . ." But then he saw another thing that drove even the thought of Dagg from his mind.

It seemed that for a moment a lull descended on him. Despite the wind and dark, his vision cleared. The stamp of thunder, the lightning's flare, and the wet pummeling of rain faded from him. To southward he could see a long flail of cloud spinning down out of the thunderheads. It was wholly black, writhing and dancing like a whipsnake upon its tail. Where it touched the Plain, great gouts of earth sprang up and whirled away.

But before Jan, between him and the storm, stood a unicorn, far away on the crest of the long gentle slope down which the band had just run. He could make out nothing more about it, neither its color nor its gender nor its age. The stormwind seemed to make its short, thick mane stream upright along its neck.

The unicorn was singing. Jan was certain of that. His body heard it through the air; it reached his hooves as a kind of trembling in the ground. It made his eyes water, his breast burn—and he wanted to follow, follow without thought, that music, wherever the singer might lead.

The unicorn turned then, westward, trotting away in a dancing stride. The low, magical singing floated back, sweeter, immeasurably sweeter than panpipes to his ears. The Serpent-cloud veered sluggishly. It seemed to hesitate, and then drifted after the retreating unicorn, docilely as a nurseling after its dam.

Jan cried out as he realized they were going. He staggered after them a few paces—and the vision ended. The rush of stormwind returned, and the lightning's clash. Feeling the wet hooves of rain upon his back, he blinked and snorted. The water stung in his nostrils, splashing his eyes.

"He's well," he heard Tek shouting beside him. "I saw him take shelter." Thunder swallowed her words. ". . . down the bank by Teki! He's safe."

Jan realized dimly she was telling him of Dagg, and felt her shouldering him back toward the gully.

"Who was it?" cried Jan over his shoulder, once he and Tek were again safely dug into the bank.

"Who?" she cried back. "I saw no one."

"The unicorn," he shouted, "at the top of the rise."

"I couldn't see the top," Tek called back at him.

"You did," cried Jan, suddenly desperate. "You must have."

The wind lashed furiously above them now. Tek bent to his ear. "What are you talking of?" she exclaimed. "I don't follow."

"You do," Jan yelled. "It was in the Vale at Moondance; it sang then, too. And in the Pan Woods—it cried out to Dagg and me and led us astray." The angry timbre of his own voice surprised him. He could not stop. "And it's been behind us, on the Plain," he cried. "You know it has. You keep slipping away from camp to look for it, or talk to it, or . . . ."

Tek did not reply.

"Now it's called away the storm." Jan demanded, "What is is? Who is is?"

"I don't know!" Tek shouted at him. "I don't know what you mean—what you've dreamed here, in the rain. . . ."

The wind tore the last of her words away. The storm had grown too wild to let them talk. She did know. She knew *something* and was not telling him. Frustration burned in him. He turned furiously away from Tek and settled himself to ride out the storm.

Eventually the gale lessened, the rolling thunder receding to north and west. Jan laid his head against the wet bank, aware for the first time how weary he was. Around him, the unicorns lay still. Gradually, the light rain subsided, and at last the sun broke through the parting clouds.

Jan stumbled to his feet, his fury spent. He heard others around him doing the same. He clambered from the gully and up the far bank, shaking off and struggling to the top of the next gentle rise. Dagg stood there. Jan went to him, and no one parted them. The storm seemed to have washed away all memory of the Renegade and Jan's disgrace.

Dagg shouldered him companionably, and the two of them stood gazing toward the west. The thunderheads hung there, small and distant now, edged red-golden by the sun.

"Look," Dagg said.

And when Jan turned, he realized for the first time that they stood in sight of the Hallow Hills.

The prince's son and the dapple colt stood watching the dusk stream over the far line of hills as the sky behind them deepened past violet to black. The band spent nearly the whole night feasting then, waiting for the ground to grow dry enough to lie upon, and eating all they could; for there would be no feasting on the morrow, the night of the nothing-moon.

Jan alternately browsed and dozed, toying with what Tek had told him during the storm. Perhaps panic *had* misled his eyes; and he had imagined it all—for he had half believed, while they had fled, that Alma had sent her Serpent-cloud for him, to strike him down for having broken the Ring and consorted with Renegades. Jan snorted then. But that was nonsense, surely, and the unicorn leading away the storm, a dream.

He slipped into genuine sleep near the end of the night, and a scant slip of waning moon appeared barely an hour before dawn. Korr roused them. They broke camp before sunup, and day broke over the Hallow Hills as the unicorns loped toward them under the horns of the moon.

Korr called a halt again, still early in the day, not a half hour's distance from the slopes. Jan watched his father scanning, testing the wind. He had ordered scouts ahead to comb for wyverns, for spring was coming in apace that year. Who knew when the wyrms might wake? The initiates he bade rest while they might, for there would be no sleep that night as they kept vigil beside the pool.

When by midafternoon the last of the prince's scouts were safely returned, having found no sign of wyverns, Korr whistled the pilgrims into line, and they entered the Hallow Hills. Their pace, a trot, seemed leisurely after so many days of hard running.

Jan found himself traversing gentle, rounded slopes newly in grass, small groves, and wide, sprouting meadows. The groves of hardwood and evergreen that they skirted looked cool and dense. After a time, Jan noticed that the hills had begun thrusting up in short cliffs. Beneath the dark topsoil, patches of pale chalk showed through.

In the late afternoon, they reached the base of a steep hillside with a narrow trail wending its face. Korr ordered them to climb. The stone proved very soft and crumbling; Jan and Dagg had to struggle to keep their footing while showers of scree from pilgrims above skidded about their hooves.

The last dozen paces of the slope were the steepest. Jan braced himself, shouldering Dagg up over the rim of the cliff, then scrambled up himself. They halted a moment, catching their breath, and Jan found they stood in a grove of hardwood trees with pale, rutted bark on twisted trunks. They were still in leaf, and their foliage had a silver cast. Jan lifted his head with nostrils wide; the scent of the trees was like mare's milk and honey.

As they moved away from the cliff's edge, deeper into the grove, Jan scented water under the fragrance of the trees and peered ahead of him. Then he caught his breath, for it lay before him, through the treeboles: the sacred pool of the unicorns, the Mirror of the Moon.

And it was round, perfectly round, twenty paces across and shallow near the banks. But it deepened at the heart, falling away in a blue cavern that went down, down it seemed into the heart of the world. No plant, no fish blotted the whiteness of its bottom or banks. No ripple marred the eye-smooth surface of the pool.

Only the flat, flaked sand at the cavern's edge fluttered in its depths like flurried snow. Jan gazed, unaware how near he had drawn. That flickering reminded him of something: birds flocking, a dance of unicorns seen from a high slope, strange stars. They seemed to form a pattern he ought to study, read. But as he started forward again, Tek moved suddenly across his path.

"Hold, prince-son," she said. "It's not yet dusk. Let the warriors prepare."

Dimly, Jan realized he had come to the grove's edge, and Dagg was no longer at his side. Jan shook his head to clear it now, and glanced about him. Warriors were stepping onto the flat, sandy bank and approaching the Mere. Initiates hung back among the trees. Jan's eyes returned to the water.

"Nothing grows there," he heard himself saying.

"Too salt," the healer's daughter said. "But with the coming of the Firebringer, they say it will grow sweet again."

Jan glanced at her.

"Come," she told him, moving away among the trees. "I'll show you the grove."

It was late afternoon as they walked among the trees. Jan gazed more closely now at their papery leaves: rounds and hearts and slender crescents, with pale undersides that reflected the light. Tek moved before him through the slim, twisted trunks and Jan followed, leisurely. The sun ran in dapples over her odd, pied coat.

"They are called milkwood," Tek was telling him, "because the sap is thick and white, sweet to the taste. The rosehips—the fruit of their flowers—drip it when ripe."

Jan was only half listening. He felt very calm, suspended almost, neither hungry nor tired now. A thick carpet of pale, wispy leaves rustled about his pasterns as he walked. Their light, rich scent hung in the air.

"It is good against toothache, pain in the bones, and some poisons."

Jan halted a moment. "They're dropping their leaves."

Tek nodded. "They do that in spring. To bloom."

Jan drew nearer to one of the trees and saw green buds upon the limbs. A breeze lifted, then fell. The slender, knotted branches shivered, and a flock of bright leaves shimmered down. The scent of resin underlay the waft of honey in the air.

"What will they look like, the flowers?" Jan asked her, trying to see past the green in the buds.

"Deep rose," the young mare answered, "or pale, with five petals, yellow at the heart."

The light wind breathed again, and the whole wood sighed. More leaves flickered, silvery in the sunlight. Jan lifted his head suddenly from the low bough he studied.

"How do you know that," he asked her, "their color and shape? You've only been here once before, and that was at first spring, too."

The young mare smiled, to herself, looking off. "My mother told me."

Jan glanced up. "How does she know?"

Tek's expression never changed. "My mother is a magicker, and knows many things."

"Like how to sing away my dreams," murmured Jan.

"Yes."

The healer's daughter still looked away. He could not see her face now, but suddenly her stance seemed very sad.

"You do not see her much, do you?" Jan ventured, trying to remember the last time he himself had seen Jah-lila. It was only that once, when he was young. "She is hardly ever in the Vale."

Since then, he had only heard of her, in whispers. Tek seemed to be looking down.

"My mother is in and out of the Vale more often than you think," she said quietly. Then, almost sharply, "But you are right. She does not come to visit me." Abruptly, she began to move away. Jan sprang to follow. Tek snorted. "Well, no matter. I do not miss her anymore."

Jan stared at her, not understanding. How could she say that? If his dam had chosen to live apart from him, he would have missed her terribly. "Why is that?" he asked of Tek.

The healer's daughter stopped then, with a sigh, as if realizing that she had said too much, and turned to face him. "Because I am not like her, little prince. When I was young, I used to tell myself, 'When I am grown, I will go to my mother and live as she lives, apart from all others, alone. But no more. I know myself better now. I am only a singer, and a warrior. Nothing will ever make me a dreamer or a magicker."

Then she moved on again, and Jan with her. They walked a little while through the trees.

"Why . . . why does she live apart?" Jan tried again. It was a question he had been wondering all his life, though he had never been able to get from anyone any answer longer than "It is her way." But Tek's reply was equally short; she did not want to talk.

"That is the prince's doing."

Jan halted, staring at her.

"Korr's . . . what do you mean?"

Tek glanced at him. "Some old falling-out between the two of them. I know nothing of it. It was before I was born. But I do know that some of it—most of it, much of it—is because my mother dreams dreams, and the prince will have no truck with dreamers. . . ."

She broke off all at once, with obvious relief, for they had come through the grove at last to the cliff's edge. The trees ended as the land sloped steeply away, then leveled off in a long, descending array of shelfland below. Sparse, stunted brushwood stood in thickets, and rivulets snaked sluggishly over the brittle white rock. Hollows of darkness showed here and there beneath the jutting shelves.

"The wyvern steps?" asked Jan, keeping his voice low. He held himself to the shadow of the trees.

Tek nodded. Her voice, too, when she spoke,

was low. "Their dens extend—probably under these cliffs as well."

Jan's glance fell to the limechalk he was standing upon. The toes of his hooves felt strange. "But they're sleeping still," he said. "The wyrms."

The healer's daughter shrugged. "We found no sign of them."

Jan gazed out over the wyvern steps. The stretch of them, away to the southeast, was vast. As he watched, the tint of sky changed, grew yellow, casting a sallow light upon the land. Jan felt a twinge between his shoulder blades. The country before him seemed unearthly still. Nothing moved among the scrub or within the dark mouths of the caves.

"Did you bury her?" Tek beside him said. Her voice was very low. Jan turned to look at her, not following. His mentor's eyes met his. "The mare," she said. "The Renegade."

Jan's forehooves slipped. He scrambled back. A little shower of stones tumbled down the white cliffside.

"I heard your hoofbeats when you slipped away," Tek was saying. "Is that where you went, back to bury her?"

A cold sensation of betrayal slid between Jan's ribs. She had known! He clamped his teeth, staring ahead as bitterness welled in his throat. Now she would give him over to Korr. He refused to care. In his father's eyes he was already hopelessly fallen.

"Aye," Jan answered defiantly. "And if I did?"

"Good," muttered the healer's daughter, looking off now. "I'd have gone with you, but you made such a noise when first we came upon her, I feared notice if we both slipped off."

It took a moment to regain his breath. Jan gazed at Tek. The young mare glanced at him.

"You are not the only one, prince-son, who breaks the Ring and follows his own heart now and again."

Jan could not recover from staring at her. He felt his jaw might brush the ground if he gaped any more. The healer's daughter turned to face him more squarely.

"Little prince," she told him, "I became a warrior as young as I could so that I might be out from under my elders' eyes and run where I willed and do as I pleased. But even before that, whenever my father caught me stepping outside the Ring, he never scolded, but only told me, 'You'll make a warrior soon enough, filly, if you stay at this clip.' "

And she laughed then suddenly, almost lightheartedly. It sounded strange in the stillness to Jan's ears. And she was laughing at him a little, it seemed, baiting him, daring him with her green, green eyes. His limbs felt weak. Abruptly, Jan felt his bravado vanishing.

"Pledge me you won't tell Korr," he whispered, for all at once hope sparked in him again. Perhaps he was not lost, after all. Perhaps in time he could win back his father's grace, if only the prince never learned of this.

The healer's daughter laughed again, more gently. "No fear. I hadn't planned to."

Jan studied her dubiously. She looked at him.

"Will you have my word on it? Here: I, Telkélla, swear."

Jan felt a sudden rush of gratitude then, and just a trace of shame. Among the unicorns of the Vale, one's truename was a secret, given at birth and known only to oneself and one's dam. Not even Korr knew Jan's truename. Yet Tek had trusted him with hers as readily as the Renegades had spoken the name of the Mother. He felt he must repay her somehow.

But Tek was already speaking. "Unless *you* speak of it, no one will ever know. But by the Beard, little prince, you were in such a froth during the storm, I thought you might babble the whole thing afterward."

She snorted, picking at the soft chalk underfoot with one hoof. Jan felt his ears burning, abashed, not quite sure whether Tek was right in thinking he had almost confessed, or because she had mistaken his desperation for terror. She gave another snort, half a laugh.

"You've been keeping yourself so docile of late—save getting yourself lost in the Pan Woods—until you spoke your father back upon the Plain, I was half afraid you'd lost your fire."

And two emotions roiled up in Jan suddenly, like wellsprings rising, overwhelming and obliterating the tranquillity that had filled him since he had entered the grove. The first was fury, fury at

Korr for all the helpless frustration he, Jan, had felt during the storm—and before that, beside the fallen Renegade when his father had simply loped away, ignoring him, as though he were *nothing*.

And the second emotion, which was for Tek, he could not even name.

"Aljan," he told her. "My truename's Aljan."

"Dark moon?" the healer's daughter said. "It suits."

He found himself gazing at her—he had been gazing at her for some time now, he realized, and could not stop—caught unexpectedly by the way the patches of black and rose in her coat mingled and interlocked. Not odd, beautiful. The suddenness of his seeing it surprised him. Why had he never noticed it before?

The color of the sky above had grown warmer, redder, and the cast of the wyvern shelves below almost coppery. Tek stood eyeing him with her green, green eyes that caught the light like gryphons' eyes, and all at once Jan felt himself flushing scarlet beneath the skin.

She tossed her head, shaking herself. "Come," the healer's daughter said. "We should go back. It's dusk."

VIGIL

Jan followed Tek back through the milkwood grove. The shadows of the trees slanted long around them, and their shadows trailed dark over the fallen leaves. Then the soil changed from grayish brown at the wood's edge to the white lime sand surrounding the pool. Dagg, already standing before the water, was glancing about anxiously. They slipped up beside him.

Jan saw other pilgrims stepping into the place about the Mere, all facing inward, ringing it round—no outward-facing sentries this night. Alma must keep them while they kept their vigil (might the wyverns not wake). The sky above, fire-streaked with gold, was mirrored in the pool.

Across the water, Korr began to speak. He told of Halla, how she had formed the Circle of Warriors in the first years after the unicorns' defeat at the teeth of the wyverns. She had made the Ring that the herd might not scatter, each running his or her own way across the Plain. It was Halla's wish that the unicorns remain a single people, whole and strong, so that one day—at the coming of the Firebringer—they might return and cast the wyverns from these hills.

But Jan found he could hardly listen. His thoughts wandered along their own path. Tek's words in the grove troubled him. Was she not, as a warrior of the Ring, bound to report him? Yet she had pledged not to. Was her breach then not as great as his?

Only the worthy, the prince was saying, only those who had kept themselves true, did Alma permit to join the Ring. As for the rest, the Ring-breakers, they were lost. As Renegades, they perished on the Plain. *Am I worthy?* Jan asked himself. *I have not been true.* Once he became a warrior, he would no longer have a colt's excuse.

He watched the sunset in the water, the gold in the sky turning to amber, then deepening to red. Streaks of shadow shaded from mauve into purple, then dusky taupe. The dusk wind lifted, stirring the grove, then soughing, died. Jan began to be able to see stars though the dim glow of sky reflected in the pool.

Teki chanted them the lay of Wenfedh, a young warrior newly returned from Pilgrimage, who had died at the talons of gryphon captors rather than forswear the Ring and betray the unicorns. The twilight turned into evening, the sky becoming deep blue and then at last true black between the stars. Silence settled; the unicorns grew still. Strange constellations lay like bright dust upon the surface of the Mere, and Jan watched them.

No moon arose. It was the night of the nothing-moon, when the moon ran mated with the sun under and around the other side of the world. On the morrow's eve, a new moon would arise, new-born, a thin crescent slip. Jan gazed intently at the still, dark water, and his tangled thoughts quieted. The night rolled by, the sky overhead wheeling slowly, ever so slowly, like a lazily circling kite.

The hour swung past midnight. Jan felt no uneasiness, no urge to sleep. His legs held firm, without stiffness, and he measured the dark, surrounding space by the little noises: a restless murmur, the scuff of hooves as someone shifted, a soft snort, a swishing of tail. Each sound fanned out, thinning, filling the night until it rebounded on the dark.

Night waned. The young hours after midnight loomed and passed. Jan found his gaze on the pool had grown deeper. Perfectly steady, he no longer needed to glance away to keep his balance or his bearings. His hooves seemed rooted to the soil, growing downward like the boles of the milkwood trees. Their savor hung on him, pervading the air.

His gaze was fixed upon the Mere, moving steadily farther into that clear deepness. He felt the woods, the others around him all falling away, and knew that he had been searching for a thing that lay hidden just beyond his gaze for a very long time. He came aware of a light, a dim glow slowly brightening that dark infinity of night. And he had existed for an age, an endless universe of time, in darkness, with only the glimmer of stars for a guide.

But now the light was coming. He felt his heart lifting, his breath quickening. The others around him—he could neither see nor hear them anymore, but he felt their kindred anticipation, scented it, tasted it almost, like the dying of the dark. The stars faded. Dawn sky blended from black to indigo, from wine to rose and apricot, then gold.

He saw something, a dark figure, but could not quite make it out. The grove around him still lay in smoky shadow, the reflected sky casting only the subtlest of light. He moved forward without thinking, nearer the water—and the vision moved. He hung over it, staring at it, holding his breath as the dawn grew gradually brighter. Then in the next moment, the vision crystalized, clarified, became—only himself, his own image reflected back at him from the surface of the Mere.

No foreseeings. No destiny. Jan felt his chest tightening until he thought his ribs would fold. His eyelids were stinging, but he refused to blink. His breath had grown ragged. He understood. He had broken from the Ring in the Pan Woods, on the first day of their journey. He had almost forgotten that. Alma had not.

He had consorted with Renegades, buried a Renegade. The Serpent-cloud had been a warning. He should have heeded it, confessed to Korr. If only Tek—but it was too late now. He was unworthy, not fit to be the prince's son, no better than a Renegade himself. The Mother-of-all had cursed him, showed him no fate upon the pool because no destiny could lie before him among the children-of-the-moon.

All around him he heard the pilgrims' voices: gasps of wonder from the initiates, sighs and murmurs as their mentors once again beheld their fates. Jan's nostrils flared. He had been holding his breath. Swiftly and without a word, he broke from the Circle and fled silently away into the trees.

Not then, but only much later—after the pilgrims had finished their beholdings and spoken their oath of fealty to the prince, heard more of Teki's lays, sharpened their hooves and horns and dipped them in the Mere, then chanted and danced to declare themselves half-grown, warriors—only then, about midmorning, did the unicorns discover one of their band was not among them.

The heady scent of the milkwood, which they had been breathing all night, had lulled them, and the languor which always follows visioning had made them slow. Dagg and Tek stared at one another and shook their heads like beasts amazed that they had not noticed him gone before. No one had seen him slip away, nor could tracks be found, for the sand of the bank was all tossed and trampled from the dance.

Korr ordered the clifftop combed, but leaves had already fallen to cover Jan's tracks. They searched and called the long hours before noon, but found no trace. Then, as they met back at the pool at midday, the whole band, Teki took the prince aside and argued with him.

The healer said, hark to the hour. By custom the band should have been back on the Plain by now. Nor might they tarry, for the pilgrims must be returned to the Vale by full moon's time, as was the Law.

And Korr, half wild, said trample the custom and the Law.

And the healer said, was the prince gone mad? Could he not feel the sun, hot as a gryphon's eye overhead? Spring came in apace this year, the grove was nearly in bloom; and it had always been held, for generations on end, that the wyverns awoke when the milkwood flowers. Who knew whether all this stirring and calling had not already wakened them?

And Korr, in a passion, answered him, let the wyverns all perish.

Then Teki said no word, but only nodded over one shoulder toward the initiates, so that Korr might take note of how huddled they stood, scanning the wood, how their skin twitched and their eyes rolled, and they started at nothing. It was the age-old terror of the wyverns, kept alive by the singers for four hundred years, that set them quailing so. Even the prince, despite his thunder, felt it.

Then the healer said, they are frightened, my prince. They fear your son has been stolen by the wyrms and that if we linger, we too shall meet the same. I fear it. Jan is a clever colt, and if he has but wandered off, lost in dreams, then surely he will find his way back to the Plain. But if he has been taken, then he is already lost, and our remaining cannot save him.

And at that, Korr bit down his anger and his fear, and bowed his head. Then he whistled the band into line once more, and they began to depart. But it was a semblance only, this seeming surrender by the prince. He meant but to see them safely to the Plain and then return, for he had vowed to himself, secretly, that he would not leave the Hallow Hills without his son.

But what no one had noticed—not he, not Teki, nor any other of the band—as they began their slow descent down the precarious cliff face, then filed at last out of sight beyond the canyon's bend, was that two of their number still searched among the milkwood trees, never having returned to the Mirror of the Moon.

No one guessed that Tek and Dagg had glanced into each others' eyes, each swearing silently to the other to find their friend despite the hour, despite the prince, despite the fear of wyverns that crawled in their breasts. Wise fear. Rash fools, they had no inkling of the prince's plan, nor had he any notion that a half-grown colt and so young a mare would dare anything so heedless or so brave.

Jan wandered through the milkwood trees. The scent of honey thickened the air. The buds upon the boughs had swelled. More leaves had fallen. He noted it all without interest. He had only a vague plan, to remain hidden in the grove till afternoon when the others would be long gone. At nightfall he would make his way back to the Plain.

He told himself he would become a Renegade. There was grass in plenty upon the Plain, and safety in his long legs if he kept his ears pricked for pards. In winter he could rove southward to the warm Summer Sea, in summer strive eastward or west to places and parts no unicorn had ever seen.

But such thoughts were no comfort to him, for he would be alone, with not even Dagg to share in the game. Always before when he had stepped outside the Ring, it had been but for a moment, an hour. And each time he had been able to return, either nipped and jaded if he had been caught, or flushed with secret triumph if the game had worked. But there would be no returning this time, for Alma had not made him like other unicorns. He saw that now.

Time passed. The sky overhead lightened past dawn into daybreak. He hurried deeper into the trees, fearing lest someone should follow him, try to force him to return. And then he came aware, presently, of another scent edging in among the honey of bursting buds and the subtle resin of bark and leaves. It was faint but pungent, like fir cones, like bitter herbs. He sniffed, trying to locate it, but the odor vanished.

Jan halted, frowning. It seemed he had smelled such a scent somewhere before—not quite the same, but similar. Somewhere. He raised his muzzle and wandered through the trees, until after a time he caught a whiff of it again. This time it held, and he followed it.

The stretch of the grove was greater than he had imagined, tending to downslope, with odd cracks here and there in the earth and little caves tunneling down. There were more of them the farther he went, and the pungent scent had grown stronger now. From several of the crannies, he noticed mist rising. It hung in the boughs of the milkwood trees.

And then he remembered the breath of fire. He and Dagg had seen it, scented it rising into the night sky in the Pan Woods, while the blue-bodied goatlings piped and danced. He halted before a crevice and leaned over, but he could see nothing past the first length of shaft. Bits of gray soil clung to the pitted stone.

But the strange mist, oddly warm and dry, made his eyes smart and his throat feel dusty. So he drew away. And then he knew nothing for a little time. He had no memory of walking; it was as if someone or something familiar bore him along without his knowing.

The next thing he was aware of was that he stood before a cave. It tunneled gradually downward into the hillside, disappearing around the bend. Wisps of scented smoke trailed upward along the ceiling like a slow, misty stream. Jan, peering into the cave's dimness, breathing its earthy air, entered its coolness as in a dream.

Pale limerock walls reflected the daylight streaming in behind. The floor looked worn, as though smoothed by water, its surface rosy crystalline, or green, or amethyst. The color changed as Jan entered deeper, as the angle of the light striking his eye altered. The floor seemed duller, somehow, softer than stone. It clicked like the substance of horn beneath his heels.

Jan picked his way down and around the turns. Every dozen paces or so, some cranny burrowed down from the surface. Wan patches of light lay on the lime walls, glimmered on the crystal floor. The meandering ramp leveled out at last into a broad, straight hall. The light was dimmer here, the walls tunneling farther from the surface overhead.

Jan moved forward, gazing dreamily about. Smaller corridors angled off on either side. All around him lay drowsy still, but even so far down, so deep in the earth, the air was not stale. A faint breeze trickled in with the light. Jan scented the air, still following the smoke tumbling languidly overhead.

He came aware of a faded odor now—it smelled barely, hauntingly sweet. Yet underneath ran a slight stench, like moldering flowers, or damp rotted leaves. The scent itself was not faint, he realized, but subtle. It had taken him a long time to discover it under the keener, more pungent odor of smoke. But it had always been there. And the scent was old, very old, though lingering.

The smoke overhead had begun to grow thicker, wider in its stream. Jan spotted where it bled into the main hall from a side corridor. He followed it. The way was narrow, very dark, and doubling back upon itself. Jan had to pick his path by feel. Then the alleyway sloped suddenly, steeply down, and angled into a larger hall.

High, shallow tunnel windows provided light, while the smoke pooled and tumbled overhead. Jan set off down the broad, well-lighted corridor still in a dream, but beginning to come to himself now, a little. The hall came shortly to an end. Jan saw ahead of him a natural doorway, and a glimpse of chamber behind.

Warm, changing light played on that snatch of wall, the white smoke spilling through the door's archway. Jan approached without volition, unaware of his own motion, as though he himself were smoke, only spilling toward the chamber, not away. He heard some slight movement beyond the door, just at the threshold of his hearing. The scent of rotting flowers had grown stronger. He reached the doorway and gazed through.

Fire lay in a golden bowl, which rested on a ledge of rock beside the far wall. The dish was circular, a pace across, and shallow like a shell. Within it, curling branches of milkwood lay upon a bed of fine gray dust. Those underneath were red and glowing, the ones on top blackened and covered with flickering tongues of flame.

At the foot of the altar lay a heap of dead milkwood branches, and upon the altar face itself, beside the bowl, a little pile of withered herbs. The wall just behind was a broad column of stone, grooved and water-stained.

Water had worn a depression in the wall overhanging the fire. The stone was eaten very thin there, translucent: Jan could see the water through the stone. The little crescent-shaped cistern was full to the brim. As he watched, a clear droplet condensed through a crack in the rim and fell into the flames with a hiss.

He had no idea how long he stood there. Time had become suspended, as it does in dreams. It seemed a long time. The room was warm, Jan realized suddenly, warmer than the cool, shaded corridors down which he had just come, warm almost as the air outside. The air above the firebowl shimmered with heat.

He watched the smoke arise and swirl about the ceiling, some of it escaping through the light well illuminating the chamber's center. It was then Jan realized that he had entered the room, skirting the sun curtain as if by instinct, staying in shadow. He stood now only a few paces from the firebowl, and felt the last of whatever influence had brought him there dissolve. He was himself again, fully aware. And then a cold, sliding voice behind him said:

"When you have had done admiring my fire, little dark thing, turn around, that I may look you in the eye."

Jan spun around. The wyvern lay on a bed of great, round stones, a sort of ground, he guessed, for sleeping. Larger than himself, larger even than Korr, the white wyrm reclined, its tail coiled langorously about itself, and forked at the end into three arrowhead stings.

Pearly, like the inside of a seashell, the creature stared at him. Its slender torso was propped on stubby forelegs, broad and clawed like a badger's, but hairless, white-skinned, and translucent in the firelight. Jan could see the fingerbones through the flesh.

The wyvern had three heads. Jan felt a shudder run through him as he realized it. The long, sinuous neck was divided near the base, with the lowest head being also the smallest. On the other side, a higher, thicker branch bore a larger head. But only the tallest, central head had spoken. The other two hissed softly, shifting and swaying. All three were looking at him.

"I said come away from my fire," it told him again, and the second added, its voice lighter than the primary's, somehow younger, "Stand in the sunlight." And when Jan hesitated an instant's breadth, the third head snapped, "Can you not understand a civilized tongue? Be quick."

The creature lay between him and the door. Jan's heart beat hard and slow inside his ribs, and his throat was desperately dry. But strangely, curiosity very nearly overrode his fear. It scarcely resembled anything he had imagined of wyverns from the singers' tales: white and sinuous, yes, but not noxious, not hideous. Very lithe and supple, rather—almost . . . almost beautiful. Jan stepped forward into the light.

"What is it?" he heard the two heads whispering. The primary head poised, eyeing him.

"What manner of creature . . . ?" the second head began, but the tallest laughed.

"A unicorn! I have not seen one alive since my babyhood four hundred summers gone. Speak, unicorn. Tell us your business and your name."

Jan felt his blood quicken. The white wyrms were sorcerers that could fell kings with a kiss. To give one his name, even his usename, would be a dangerous thing.

"Speak," the third, smallest head hissed at him. "Your name."

Sunlight was dazzling him; he could scarcely see for the glare. He shifted his stance till one eye moved into shadow.

"Do not approach," the second head started, but the great one snapped at it.

"Oh, peace," it ordered, languidly. "A little silence."

The wyvern reared up, flexing and extending both powerful, stunted forepaws so that only a toe or two remained in contact with the ground. It was, it seemed, less looking at him now than scenting him. Jan noted the sickle-shaped nostrils, the catfish whiskers, and wondered how well this wyvern could see him out of strong light. He took another sidelong step, getting his other eye out of the glare.

"I have heard," it began, almost companionably, "that the unicorns now live in a valley far to the south. They are ruled by a prince, are they not, a black prince?"

It settled back upon its bed of stones. Its three heads tilted and bobbed. Jan gazed at it and racked his brains. How to get past? He needed a stratagem, for it was huge. He could never hope to best it in a fight.

The wyvern did not seem to mind his silence. "You, too, are dark, little unicorn," it resumed presently. "You would not by chance be some relation of his—his nephew, perhaps? Perhaps his *son.*"

If that last word was accented, ever so slightly, Jan hardly heard. His gaze had fixed on the wyvern's tail. Its triple-barbed tip twitched and lashed as it spoke, sometimes coiling and knotting back on itself. Above, its three heads lazily bobbed and swayed. He found their ceaseless weaving fascinating.

"You are admiring my three heads," it said suddenly. The flanking two hissed and intertwined, whispering to each other now. The central one continued mildly. "You know something of wyverns? It is unusual, yes. But I am very old. Only the very old among us grow more than one head."

Its voice was strange, hollow, oddly modulated. It shifted up and down scales weirdly, invitingly. Abruptly, Jan shook himself, on guard against its spells.

"Yes, I am old," the wyvern sighed, "and only the king has seen more years. Lynex has lived to seven heads."

Lynex. Jan felt a bolt go through him. Surely not that same Lynex from the old lays? The wyvern paused, surveying him, he guessed, to see whether its wordspell was having an effect—and felt a small triumph to see its flash of disappointment. But the wyvern hid it swiftly, and resumed.

"I was not sleeping, just now when you entered. Oh, no. I do not sleep much in winter, as others do. Do you know why we sleep the winters by, most of us? Too cold." It shimmered, shrugging. "And not enough food in the cold season, too."

It nodded past him toward the golden carrying bowl. There was no wind in the still chamber, but Jan could feel the fire's heat along his coat in gusts.

"But I am mistress of the wyverns' fire. The king

granted me this honor when I was no more than a slip, barely hatched, not long after we won these shelves for our own from you unicorns."

Jan felt a spark of anger then. Almost, it overrode his fear. The other's eyes darted wickedly, as if expecting him to understand something that he did not. The firelight glinted in them, and ran over the walls in watery streams.

"Lynex's reward for my part in the battle."

The wyvern laughed suddenly, throwing back all her heads, her mouths gaping wide, and Jan caught a glimpse of her teeth for the first time: like ice-splinters, or fishes' spines, rows of them.

"There, my little cloven-footed visitor. Now do you understand who it is who commands you to speak—or does my greatness overawe you?"

Jan found his voice.

"You are a wyvern, hatched just before your people drove mine from our homeland through trickery and deceit. *That* is all I know of you."

He saw the other's eyes flash then. She reared again.

"Oh, you are full of contempt, are you, little four-foot, for me and my kind? Because we use stratagems to gain our ends when it suits us."

"Proud beasts!" the second head spat. "Do you think that you yourselves are above such games—that none of you ever harken to the whispers of power?"

The littlest head spoke now in a voice gone suddenly quiet, almost sweet. "Did your own princess not cut down her father, seizing his place four hundred years past, just before we took possession of these hills?"

Jan stared at her, and felt his blood burning. That she could even speak of such a thing! But he had no time to make reply.

"Has your own father not held you back from initiation because he fears you? You are cleverer than he, and see much he cannot or will not see."

Jan clenched his teeth. *Lies, all of it.*

"And does the prince's mate not scheme against him by urging you to follow your own heart, not his commands. . . ?"

"Not so!" cried Jan. "Halla was a brave princess and a true warrior who struck in her own defense against the king, who was mad with a wyvern in his ear and fell dead when the thing had eaten out his reason." He drew breath, shaking with rage. "And as for Ses, and Korr my father . . . ."

"Ah." The wyvern smiled. Very white she looked suddenly, very cool and deadly. Her teeth snapped, still smiling. "So you *are* the prince's son."

Jan choked to a halt, startled, staring. The wyvern's gaze had grown keen now, her eyes like polished stone. The flanking heads growled, deep in their throats, but the main one snaked closer to him.

"Listen to me, Aljan son-of-Korr, did you think I would not know you? That I had drawn you down into my den with a spell of fire to no purpose?"

Her whiskers bristled. The ruff of gills on her three heads spread. Jan felt astonishment flood him. She knew his name, his own truename, and had known it all along. Fear sprang into his mind again, cold as river ice. A wyvern magicker held him in her power.

"I am the mistress of mysteries," she whispered. "I gaze into fire and much I see there. I know your people dream of a great hero, one who would make war on the wyverns and drive us from our dens. . . ."

"The Firebringer," breathed Jan.

"Your name for him is unimportant," the wyvern snapped. "I care only that he is to be color-of-night—a black warrior such as this Korr who rules you now."

"My father," murmured Jan. Did she know, did she speak the truth? Was Korr to be the Firebringer?

"It is he; it *must* be," her third head was muttering. "What other unicorn is color-of-night?"

"And yet, for a long time, I was not sure." The second head mused now, seemingly more to itself than to him. "Though I watched him—and lately I have been at great pains to thwart him—for the patterns in the sky have told me this hero's time is coming, very soon."

The central head was looking at him.

"Yes, I can read the stars," she said, "though their meaning is often veiled. And there are other powers within my skill. When upon my fire I lay certain herbs, I can walk in others' dreams."

"Dreams," murmured Jan, and just for an instant her voice became so familiar, eerily so, he could have sworn he had heard it somewhere, somehow before. "I dreamed once, in a gryphon's eye. . . ."

He remembered now, with perfect clarity, that dreamlike trance.

"Dreamed I saw a fair serpent charming a hawk. Was it you?" He turned to the white wyrm again suddenly. "You who spoke in the gryphon's dream?"

The wyvern laughed. "I have seen many things gazing into my fire. One of them is how close the Gryphon Mountains lie to your Vale. And the gryphons are jealous. Shreel, the blue female—I spoke in her dream of the glory to be had if she and her mate destroyed the black prince of the unicorns."

Jan felt himself shivering, with revulsion, not fear. "We defeated your wingcats," he told her. "Killed them both."

The wyvern shrugged.

"And the pans?" Jan demanded suddenly, remembering now the sting of stones, the whistles of warriors, branches whipping, and horns crying in pursuit.

"I told the goatlings when your pilgrimage would pass." She smiled. "But my powers lie not only in the reading of stars and the directing of dreams. I can call things and conjure things, given time: raise wind and bring weather. . . ." Her long, sinuous necks shifted, swaying. She hummed a little, almost crooning.

"The Serpent-cloud," cried Jan, softly. His limbs prickled, momentarily weak. "You called the storm upon the Plain."

The wyvern's middle head chuckled. "Clever. No. I did not make it—but I did coax one wheeling funnel of darkness to dance your way."

"We outran it," Jan answered, defiant. "It passed us by."

"Well," the wyvern said. "I am almost glad, for that has enabled you to come to me."

She shifted position, coiling herself more tightly about her sleeping-stones.

"Smug unicorns," her third head muttered, "thinking yourselves so secret and so safe. Did you think we do not know what you unicorns do, that you come each year at borning spring into our hills?"

Our hills, *our* hills, she called them.

"Come for your rites by the poison pool," the second head added. "We find your marks, your hoofprints above the banks, traces of your passage along the paths."

The main head rested now upon the stones, seemingly unconcerned, letting the others talk.

"We know about your *Circle*," the little head murmured, the last word hissed. "How you, all of you, pledge yourselves to it and serve it. And I know the reason you are with me now, young hothead, is that you are *outcast*."

That last she spat, crackling with contempt. Jan felt his bravado vanish instantly. Shame scathed him like a scourge. It was the truth. She spoke the truth. Her words needed no spell now to catch him in their teeth. The wyvern laughed.

"Yes, little mud-prince, no more your father's heir. That, too, has been my doing, in a way. Your hasty temper hardly needs much prodding, but I have teased it when I willed."

He stared at her, and felt again all at once that wild hotheadedness coiled inside him like a snake.

"Oh, yes, Aljan. I have been watching you for a very long time. Did you think I would not keep one trick in the back of my teeth in case all my others against your father failed?"

She had raised her central head again, and turned it slightly, eyeing him. Beneath that malevolent gaze, Jan felt his resistance vanishing. The two flanking heads chuttered and hissed.

"Do you not remember all the dreams that I have sent you?"

And the memories came then, unclouded, unimpeded at last, and terrifying: a longfish swimming in the water, a winged serpent that hatched out of the moon, salamanders that burst bright into flame—and a dozen others such as he had had before the coming of Jah-lila. But now the passage of time and the white wyrm's words, her burning smoke and Jan's own efforts to recall had at last swept all the wild mare's protections away.

The wyvern's eyes blazed into his.

 "*Dreams,* Aljan, to wean you away from the

unicorns and win you to my cause, though you did not until this moment know it. The length of your life I have prepared for your coming. And now, at last, at long last, my unicorn, you are here."

Jan forced himself to speak, forced his lips and teeth and tongue to move, for he felt paralyzed, exactly as he had in the gryphon's cave, as he had in the first moments of the pans' attack. He knew even now that he must fight, fight the urge to surrender to her spells. He could not take his eyes from the white wyrm before him.

"What do you want of me?" he managed.

"Ah," the wyvern said, and her other heads echoed, "Ah." She smiled. All three of her faces smiled. "I know your heart, Aljan the dark moon. And in your heart you are a trickster. Not so?"

He found himself nodding, just barely nodding before he was even aware, and he realized, dimly, he must already have slipped a little under her spell. She settled herself.

"Well, so am I a trickster, a plotter. . . ."

"A betrayer," added Jan—*magicker, liar, dreamstalker*—forcing himself desperately to speak, act, think of his own volition, not hers.

"Yes. I tried to reach your father once, before your birth, Aljan, when Korr was young and not yet prince, and I had perceived only the vaguest of forebodings among the stars."

The wyvern's gaze turned inward now, her necks, her tail knotting and unknotting.

"I tried to send him a dream to ruin him, send him running wild Renegade across the Plain, that this hero-to-be might never come and trouble my people with war; but I could not reach him. His mind was closed to me, safe within your Ring of Law."

Her eyes came back to Jan, a hunter's eyes.

"Your father is no dreamer, Aljan. And so for years I was frustrated, uncertain whether this young black prince was to be our starspoken enemy. And I was unable to strike at him, either, even when his yearly Pilgrimage brought him so *close*."

Her eyes flashed and her three jaws snapped. Jan shivered.

"For the winters here have been freezing chill these last ten years, spring's warmth not in till long after equinox. And though each time he has come I have been awake, here below, I dared not leave my fire untended, nor could I rouse my people from their winter sleep."

Again that flash of eyes, that triple snap.

"But then . . . ." Her tone was silken, and suddenly the scent of woodsmoke in the air seemed sharper, the room closer, the light dimmer and the white wyrm herself even paler and more opalescent. "Then I saw, not many seasons past, a mare in labor under a dark moon: the prince's mate. And I knew this prince would have a son. . . ."

"A dreamer born," the third head hissed.

The second laughed. "One whose mind was not closed to me."

"One who would *not* keep himself safe within the Ring of Law."

She slithered toward him suddenly, rearing up, her cut-jewel eyes measuring him and all her heads weaving upon their slender stalks. Jan stumbled back. The rays of the light well glided over him and glanced in his eyes.

"I want you to play another trick, Aljan. For me—a little trick. Only that."

Jan stared at her. Her shimmer dazzled him. "What manner . . . of trick?" The words seemed to drag from his teeth, so slowly. The effort of speech had become almost pain. His thoughts had blurred, and her voices seemed to wash over him in waves. He listened, only half understanding what she said.

"Our king is old, Aljan, and has no heirs. No need, he says, for he will live another hundred years at least. But I am not content. Lynex lets our people languish. Too much sleep has made them slothful. The poison in their tails is weaker. . . ."

"Some . . ." the second head broke in. The wyvern shifted on her spot. "*Some* even hatch with no stings on their tails at all—blunt tips, nothing!"

Her central head champed its teeth, the little one muttering. "Such freaks would have been eaten at birth when I was young. But the king grows lax. A weak people are easier for him to manage in his age. Well."

Once more she shifted.

"I would make my people great again. I would

share fire among all the dens as when first we came here. The wyverns must breed in winter as we once did, and the weak be eaten, if our line is to regain its vigor. Now only the piddling summer eggs hatch, and no fruit comes of an autumn tryst. . . ."

"But only because of the *cold*," the second head hissed. "With fire, I could . . . ." She broke off. "Ah, but the king will not listen to me."

"I want you to return to your father, Aljan," the white wyrm said suddenly. Her eyes had come back from their distance now. The central head spoke. "Explain your absence somehow. Tell them you have seen a marvel, our dens deserted, or all the wyverns dead of plague. Tell them anything, but make them follow."

Jan watched her, helpless now to move or speak. He wanted to run, turn away, shake his head in flat refusal, but his body would not obey. And he was outcast. *Outcast*. He could never go back. She laughed softly.

"It is our king's custom to be first out of the dens in spring, to go hunting and bring back the season's first catch: red meat for his people upon their awakening. But how if I were to seize that right? The people love me, support me. They would proclaim me his heir. Then he *must* listen."

Again her eyes found him.

"You must lead your people away from the poison pool, Aljan. My people still fear that place—superstitious fools! Lead your father and his band into the canyon below the cliff. It is a dead end, with sides too steep for your kind to scale."

She preened herself a moment, fretfully.

"I, meanwhile, will rouse my people. They sleep lightly this year, with the spring come in so early and so mild." She laughed, all three heads shaking, their sliding notes hollow and strange. "To kill the black prince of the unicorns and outstrip my own king in a single stroke. Will that not be, little trickster after my own heart, the finest game of all?"

Jan stared at her across the well of sunlight. Firelight played over the minute scales of her delicately tinted skin. They flaked off along her underside as she slid along the floor. It must be these, he found himself thinking suddenly, irrelevantly, packed down and hardened for centuries, that formed the crystalline surface of the tunnel floors.

His captor grew impatient for his reply. She spat, "Surely you can feel no loyalty to them, pompous unicorns, the very ones that cast you out?"

The truth in her words mocked at him. No, he was not like other unicorns, could not keep to the old ways, to Halla's Circle, though his father's pride and the love of Alma depended on it. The white wyrm coiled about her bed of stones, looking at him, laughing at him with her three pairs of cut-jewel eyes.

Jan could not recall ever seeing a creature more beautiful, though there nagged somewhere at the back of his mind the notion that she ought to have seemed hideous. Why? For she was pure, admirably pure, without a twinge of conscience or shame.

"Serve me, Aljan," her little head hissed. "Once we have destroyed the unicorns, I will let you go—off across the Plain to run wild Renegade if you will. Or even," her voice grew sly, "back to your Vale. Who would know, with all the others dead, that anything you chose to tell them was not the truth? *You* would be prince, then, little darkling. *You* would rule the unicorns. . . ."

Something struck him then, dimly, through the fog. Why was she so importunate? And then that, too, came to him—*because time is slipping away. It must be noon by now, or past, and the unicorns preparing to quit the pool. Because I am the last trick she has against my father. Without me she will never get him into that dead-end canyon. Her people are afraid to go near the poison pool.*

And without me to lead the unicorns into her trap, she will never have her bold stroke to outshine the king, to seize his place in her people's hearts and come to power. I am the spark to all her kindling. Without me, her great scheme becomes only ashes and dust. I have only to refuse her, and she shall be undone. I have only to refuse.

But he could not refuse. For she held his name, like a mouse struggling in her teeth. Aljan, Aljan—every time she said the word, he felt himself sink deeper in her power. He was tangled, frozen; he could not get free. Her spells had knotted round him like a snake. But she seemed oddly unaware how nearly he was hers—and then he realized he stood in shadow now. She could hardly see him.

"How may you deny me?" her central head grated. Her tone had grown darker. She hissed with frustration. "Look what I have offered you: power, freedom, the death of your enemies. Unicorns! I know your kind to the marrow of the bone. When I was barely hatched, I fed upon the wit of one mightier than you, foal princeling. Do not tell me I do not know the things that tempt a unicorn."

Her words, like a thunderclap, brought Jan sharp awake. The cold coils that had trammeled his mind fell away. He stared. This one, this great three-headed thing, had been the little slip to gnaw away the mind of Jared the king half a hundred generations gone? She. *She* had done?

A blazing anger rose in Jan, and the last of the white wyrm's spell dissolved in its heat. His jaw tightened; his body tensed. He tossed his head, his nostrils flaring. He was Jan, the son of his people's prince, and not some wyvern's gamepiece. Eyeing her ice-white, reptilian form, he felt himself growing dangerous.

"What will you give me?" said Jan suddenly. "What will you give me in exchange for the unicorns?" He picked up his hooves and set them down again, restlessly, for a sense of power had flowed into him. He could not keep still. The wyvern cocked her heads, clearly surprised.

"What I have said . . ." she began.

"No," Jan told her. "My freedom? The leadership of the unicorns? Those things I will have anyway, if I do as you say." He sidled, dancing. "You must give me another thing—to make this worth my game. Another thing, mistress of mysteries."

The white wyrm lay silent, eyeing him suspiciously. Jan knew it must be plain to her that he no longer lay beneath her spell; but it did not matter. He had her. She needed him. She *must* agree.

And if he could stall her, dicker with her long enough to let the unicorns depart the Hallow

Hills, if he could keep her from rousing her people for only so long—a weary sense of finality overcame him now—then it did not matter what happened to him after she found out he had been gaming her.

The wyvern shrugged after a moment, her smallest head snapping its teeth. "Oh, very well, little unicorn," she muttered. "What will you have? I will give it to you if I must—only because it pleases me." Her central head added sharply, "But be brief. Our time is short."

Time, time, thought Jan, what thing might he ask her for that would take the most time? A mystery. One of her mysteries—but which? How to read the stars? Only there were no stars, for it was still broad day. How to raise wind and bring weather? But here below, out of sight of the sky . . . .

His gaze strayed to the firebowl, burning red flags in a golden shell. The air rippled and distorted above it, threads of black smoke rising and twining, then thinning out into a gray haze near the chamber's ceiling. The wet pillar of stone gleamed behind the heat shimmer. Jan returned his gaze to the wyvern.

"Tell me of fire."

"Ah." The wyvern forced a smile. "You are ambitious, little darkling, and far more clever than I thought. Knowledge is a greater tool than mere glory. Very well. I will begin to show you. Then you will run my errand for me. But we can start the lesson now."

Her flanking heads hissed, as if to make some protest, but the great head warned them both to silence with a glare. She left her bed of sleeping-stones and slithered past Jan to the slab of rock where the firebowl rested. Jan realized with a start that his path to the doorway now lay clear. The wyvern's back was turned to him.

But he dared not flee, for even if he were able to outrun her, much less find his way to the surface again, her clamor would doubtless rouse her people, and that he could not afford. The wyverns must continue to sleep until the unicorns were clear of the hills.

He heard a sound in the passageway suddenly, just a small, soft sound: a scrape, a scuff, far down the corridor outside. He froze, listening, his skin gone cold, but no further noise came to his ears. The chill faded. It must have been nothing, a bit of earth shifting. He turned back toward the white wyrm and her fire.

But then, just as he was turning, another thing caught his attention. His gaze fell on the wyvern's sleeping ground, and for the first time he realized what it was. Not stones, not great round stones, but eggs, a double-dozen of them, melon-sized. They shone with the same milky translucence as the wyvern herself, as the chamber's floors, as the passageways. Each globe was mottled like a moon, and within each Jan saw a tiny wyrmlet coiled.

The wyvern had half turned to look at him. This time her smile was real. "Yes, eggs." She crooned now, all three heads at once. "Winter eggs—the first such our warren has seen in almost four hundred years. And ready to hatch now, soon. Soon. The king's and mine."

Her smiles deepened. Her teeth glistened.

"I am the king's concubine—though always he has visited me only in autumn, thinking to avoid heirs that way." Her whiskers twitched. "But I am the mistress of the wyverns' fire, and I have not been cold this winter. Now my people will see for themselves how our breed may be improved."

She chuckled, hissed; but her smile spoiled after a moment, her tone growing impatient. Jan tore his gaze away from the translucent eggs to look at her.

"But come now. Enough. I will show you the fire."

Jan turned and went to join the white wyrm at the bowl.

"This, then, is flame," she told him, tossing a dry branch onto the twigs. They no longer burned now, only glowed. Jan drew up beside her, watching close. The new wood smoked, then white flames licked at it, the branch curling and blackening as the fire caught. "You must feed it wood," the wyvern said. "Dry wood is best."

Jan nodded. He had seen fire in the Pan Woods. He already knew it ate wood, and dry grass as well. The sorceress shifted impatiently. Her words were quick, half whispered. He watched the twigs she scattered crackle and burn.

"It must be tended," she told him, "like a hatchling, or it dies."

Hatchlings, thought Jan, and stole another glance back over one shoulder at the eggs. Another slight sound from the hall again—very faint, just on the edge of his hearing. *Earth, earth shifting, and no more,* he told himself. He knew in his bones it could not be wyverns. The wyverns slept. He turned back to the wyrm.

She arranged the dry, burning twigs over the coals with a moldery wet one; he noticed that it did not catch, only smoked a little, thickly. Jan stood fascinated. Her third head took a sprig of leaves and brushed the scattered ash back into the heart of the flame.

"A thick bed of ash will keep fire hot," she continued. "Sweep ash over the coals to keep them warm overnight—but not too much, too long, or you will smother them. Fire must have air. It breathes. It is alive."

Alive? thought Jan. And a little thought sprang into his mind, bright, burning like the flame. *If fire is alive, then it can be killed.* He glanced sidelong at the white wyrm, but she was studying the fire, its dancing flickers and rising tendrils of smoke.

"What else kills it?" he asked, keeping his voice low and steady.

The wyvern shrugged. "Earth kills it. A sudden gust of wind can snuff it. Or rain." *Yes. Rain.* He remembered the rain in the Lay of the Unicorns. She glanced at him. "We keep it below, protected from wind and rain."

Jan glanced at the crescent cistern above the bowl. "But near water."

The wyvern laughed. "Ah, clever, Aljan. And how if a spark overleapt the bowl? The crystal floor of our dens is flammable, the oil of our skins volatile. Flame would run along our caverns faster than we could slither to escape." A low laugh. "It happened once."

She smiled slyly.

"In the beginning, when first we lived here, the king shared fire among us all. Every chamber had its hearth. Eggs hatched in all seasons, and no one slept. But all the while, the trails were building up—within a few years all our passages were crystal-coated.

"Then one day a torch fell—some servant in the king's room—no one knows. That whole quarter of the warren went up. The king escaped, but many did not. We tore down the ceilings of connecting passageways to seal the wing. It smoldered for days.

"Afterward, Lynex ordered all fire either killed or confiscated, and put it into my keeping as a sacred charge. . . ."

Jan stared unseeing into the dancing flames, and it seemed he could almost see what the wyvern described to him, behold it happening that moment, vivid as a dream.

"But what *is* fire?" he found himself demanding, interrupting the white wyrm. "Where does it come from?"

The mistress of mysteries bent her head to his ear.

"Sunstuff," she whispered. "The stuff of lightning flash in storms. Starstuff—our god. It can kill or quicken eggs to life: a weapon or a friend. It is Magic. It is Power, the source of all our sorcery. We worship it."

She was looking at him from the corners of her eyes.

"One can even see visions in the fire, if one is a dreamer or a sorceror. Look, look into the fire, little unicorn. Look closer. Closer."

Her voice had grown sly, but Jan hardly noticed. He leaned forward. The heat shimmer above the flames was like water rippling, like the stirring beneath the surface of the Mirror of the Moon. The wyvern's mocking laughter haunted softly through the room. She lifted a clump of herbs from beside the firebowl. They were small, withered pods with wispy spires on the underside.

"What are those?" he asked.

"Rosehips," the wyvern said, "the fruit of the milkwood tree. We gather them in autumn." She tossed them onto the fire. "They give a sweet smoke to bring one dreams."

Jan watched the round seed cases fall among the burning twigs. Soon they began to smolder, to send up thick, twining tendrils of smoke, pearly white mixed with bluish gray. The pale smoke had the heavier, milder fragrance, smooth and soothing; the darker, thinner threads had the keener scent. It stung his eyes.

Jan realized he had leaned far forward over the rosehips even as the wyvern had moved back out of their vapor. His face, his throat and nostrils tingled. A trembling began in the center of his limbs, made him feel at once weak and utterly unbendable, rooted to the stone. The sensation spread to his chest and ribs.

His senses were growing very acute suddenly. Before, he had not noticed the sound of fire. Now it fascinated him—a thick hissing, almost a thrum, like sea surf, a slow, arresting roar. He began to distinguish licks of color in the flames, greens and reds, pale violets. They flickered and danced.

Behind him he heard the three heads of the wyverns arguing.

"Why have you told him our secrets, of fire?" That was the second head, impatient but controlled.

"No matter." The central head, softly. "He's no more than a prit, a child. And he'll have no time to make use of what we've given him, even if he understood . . . ."

"And why the rosehips?" the little head cut in. "Their influence is always uncertain. They may put him in such a stupor he'll be no use to us at all."

"What choice had we?" the great head snapped. "We are out of time. And how was I to know he would be strong enough to throw off a wordspell? Only the fire seems to have any power over him."

"I say pounce on him now and be done," the third head muttered.

"*Patience*. We've other plans for him."

Jan did not mind their words. He knew he ought to, somehow, but he could not manage it. The wyvern's voices remained a faintly distracting background noise.

"Hist, be still." That was the second head again. "He's not quite under yet."

Under what? Jan wondered briefly, and could not care. He had the feeling that he must watch, watch very carefully now, as if this were the most important lesson of his life and he must memorize it all the first time, for it would not come again.

Yet at the same time he was vaguely aware that presently he must act. Watching the fire was important, surpassingly important, but it would end soon. He mulled over what he might be expected to do then, and had not a clue. No matter. A plan would come to him, or not, just as it chose. Things were moving so slowly now. There was time enough.

"I say slay him," the third head hissed. The thin, sharp sound of its voice fizzed on the air. "Our eggs are but a day or two from hatching; perhaps only hours. Red meat to nourish our little prits—and meat improves with age."

Jan admired the glow of the charring rosehips. They did not seem to burn. *Winter eggs,* he thought. *Little poison-prits.* Heirs to the king that would have no heirs. What had Lynex done, all these hundreds of years? *Pashed all the eggs of his mates to bits before their hatching.*

"*Fah.*" The wyvern's second head scoffed at the third. "If we killed this unicorn now, I can well guess where the greater part of the flesh would go—down your greedy gullet."

"Only a little," the little head sniffed. "What could be spared. The winter has been long. I'm ravenous."

The second head did not reply. Jan listened without interest. The fire was absorbing his whole attention. But he had begun to feel that time was starting to slip away. He sought to rouse himself from the torpor now creeping over his limbs, tried to lift his head away from the heat, but the vapors were making him slow. His limbs refused to move. He made to speak—how slowly the words formed in his mind.

"Is this . . . ." He had to pause, draw a breath heavy with smoke. His throat burned. "Is this the only fire the wyverns have?" He could not seem to turn his head. The words did nothing to lift the spell.

"Yes," the wyvern's central head replied, raising its voice, "save for the king's. He keeps his own small torch with him. The king, you see, must never sleep." She laughed, mocking. "And he thinks to keep himself safe from my magic that way. But his puny brand does not make half the flame my firebowl does."

Jan felt himself falling back into the fire, felt it consuming his thoughts. He had scarcely been able to drag his mind away to listen to the white wyrm's reply. Behind him, the heads were arguing, hissing and snapping.

"Fool, would you undo all that we have worked for? Once we have taken the prince of the unicorns and his band, there will be plenty of red meat—for our hatchlings and your greedy mouth as well." A simper, a smile. "I shall see that the king gives us this one, though, this little dark one specifically. Only the best meat for my prits."

He knew then that his time truly was out. But his muscles were melting, his head drooping, chin bowed to his chest. The heat grew fierce. His body prickled with sweat. An updraft from the coals lifted his forelock, flinging it back gently from his brow. He closed his eyes.

Even with his eyes closed, it seemed he could still see the flames—see into them as in a dream; looking deeper and deeper, merging more and more into their changing dance. Searching for something. Searching as others had been searching—for him.

He came aware then, in a twinge that was not sufficient to wake him, that others had been searching for him, many others of his band. But that was hours ago. Now there were only two. Two searching above ground, below ground. It was all the same.

"Just a few moments more," the great head was murmuring, "and the rosehips will make him a slave to our command."

Jan's nose was now well back from the lip of the bowl, below the rising smoke. The air he breathed felt cooler, more clean. His senses seemed to be clearing. The heat upon the rest of his face intensified. He laid his ears back along his skull.

His thoughts had grown dim. He felt his horn's tip touch the far rim of the bowl, and realized distantly that bright flame must be licking its long, spiral shaft. He felt no pain, only heat like the sun. The white wyrm's triple laugh echoed, sounding oddly faint and farther than it should have. Jan's consciousness was ebbing, his ears muffled in wool, his limbs slipping away.

"Not long now," the wyvern was murmuring. "See how he faints over the flame."

Jan came to himself suddenly at a soft, crackling hiss. The scent of singed hair filled his nostrils. He felt a sharp pain across his brow and realized as he started up that his forehead had touched the curved lip of the bowl, his heated sweat turning to steam. The pain made him suddenly aware of himself again, gave him the use of his limbs. He heard the wyvern sliding toward him across the crystal floor.

It came to him then, all in a breath, what must happen now. The wet, stained wall above the fire-bowl gleamed, the pearly, translucent pocket in its stone catching the firelight like a gryphon's eye. It seemed to glow. Beneath the wyvern's subtle, pervasive sweetness, beneath the pungency of rosehips and flame, the scent of water had grown suddenly strong.

Without another moment's thought, he sprang forward, rearing, bracing his forehooves on the altar's edge. The branches in the bowl of fire had died again to coals, the blackened rosehips crumbled to ash. Jan champed his teeth, clenching shut his eyes against the updrafts of heat, and brought his horn down in a hard blow against the wall above the fire.

"Hold!" cried one of the wyvern's heads. Another cried, "What does he do?"

The thin stone shattered like an old seashell. Chips of crystal flew. Jan felt bits striking against his forehead, his closed eyelids. The point of his horn struck the hard stone at the back of the crescent pool.

"Stop!" the wyvern shouted. "Are you mad?" He heard the soft scratch of her belly scales upon the floor.

Jan opened his eyes and shied to one side as water rushed from the breached cistern. The hot coals below sizzled, overwhelmed. White licks of fire leapt roofward, vanishing, as bits of twig and dead embers rode the surge, washing over the rim of the firedish and spilling to the floor. The rest swirled sluggishly about the bowl.

The chamber stood all at once in smoky dimness. The white wyrm gave a triple shriek. Jan turned his head. She sat transfixed, her pale form indistinct in the sudden gloom. Her voices rang out again, strangled.

"What have you done?" cried the central head; and the second, "He has killed the god! All our magic, all our power—gone." The third head shouted, "Murderer!"

The wyvern lunged. Jan sprang away, his limbs still giddy from the rosehips' breath. The wyvern missed him by two paces—then he realized it was not he she had sprung at. She darted to the altar, searching frantically among the sodden twigs. But the fire was dead past saving. Her three heads turned on him like goshawks. He made out the glinting of her cut-jewel eyes.

Too late he realized he had missed his chance—he should have fled while she had been distracted. Jan found himself in a corner, one wall crowding against his flank. The white wyrm reared before him, her whiskers bristled, her gill ruffs spread. Her necks stretched wide; her pale jaws gaped. Her teeth like broken birds' bones gleamed.

Jan squared himself to fight.

Jan faced the wyvern across the narrow space, her body poised, her eyes colorless in the hazy dimness. His blood felt slow and heavy from the rosehips' breath. She snapped at him. He dodged, the wall crowding his flank. The wyvern smiled, her rosy, double tongues darting among her needle teeth. The fingers of her foreclaws twitched.

"Oh, did you think to thwart me, Aljan?" she whispered. The chamber echoed in the dark. "Then you misjudged. So my fire is gone, and my magic, too. But I am angry now, Aljan." Her heads hissed, sizzling. "And there was always more to me than magic."

He was lost. He knew it. He had neither the size nor the strength to defeat her, and she had him cornered. But he would fight. He was a warrior, the prince-son of the unicorns, and he meant to go down fighting. There would be no songs to mark his death; and none of his people would even know. But he had saved Korr and the others of the band. It was noon—they were safe out of the hills by now, and none of the rest of it mattered.

Above him the wyvern loomed. She came toward him slowly. Then suddenly behind her, beyond the entry to the chamber, Jan heard a scrabbling of earth and a wild, high shrill. The note was echoed by another—the battle whistle of a warrior. The white wyrm started, snapping around. Jan heard a clatter of hooves on the crystal floor. The wyvern reared, recoiling, as a form—two forms—glanced through the well of light.

He caught glimpses then of rose and black, of dusty yellow shading into gray. He heard the snort of breath and the sound of struggle. The mist of rosehips rose in his mind, and he was a long time recognizing Tek and Dagg.

They were fighting in and out of the suncurtain now. He saw his shoulder-friend lunge, miss, and lunge again. The wyvern's long, sinewy necks darted, teasing them. Her jewel eyes glinted. Tek reared, panting, but could not seem to land a blow. The wyvern dodged, her hide throwing off brilliant flashes in the sunlight: blue-green, amber, yellow, mauve.

"The light," Jan heard himself crying, and his voice sounded different—deeper?—or as if there were another voice in it besides his own. "Drive her into the shade," he cried. "These wyverns have no eyes to pierce the dark."

One of the wyvern's heads turned, her whiskers bristling, her nostrils flared, and struck at him. Jan shied, circling the shaft of light. He came around and faced the wyrm. Tek and Dagg had forced her out of the sunlight. Her back now pressed the wall.

Dagg stumbled. Jan saw him lose his footing on the crystal floor. The wyvern lunged, snarling, and struck him a glancing blow with one badger-like forepaw. Dagg rolled, scrambling to his feet, then suddenly lunged and caught the wyrm's smallest head by the throat. The wyvern shrieked. On the other side, Jan glimpsed Tek fastening into the second head's ruff. The central face rose over Jan.

"Well, little darkling." She was hard-pressed, but she mocked him still. Her claws took powerful sweeps at Tek and Dagg. "So it is only you and I now, again."

Her breath came short, though her eyes were jeering. The smallest head continued to shriek.

"Your friends fight well—but even if they kill both my little heads, you will still have *me* to deal with."

From the tail of her eye, Jan glimpsed the whipping and coiling of the wyvern's necks. Tek and Dagg were being shaken, their forehooves lifted from the ground.

"Yield to me. You cannot win." The wyvern held her main head high, just out of reach. She laughed. "Betray your friends—*now,* Aljan, before I shake them off."

The smoke of rosehips still mingled in his blood. Despite himself, Jan felt her wordspell taking hold again. Her cut-jewel eyes had fixed on him. Pale, with an inner fire they shone, marvelously, malevolently inviting. And he knew that she was lying; yet it didn't seem to matter. Jan felt himself growing lost.

"Yield, little princeling. Yield," she whispered, moving toward him. "Help me to slay your friends. Even these two will be of use to me against my king. And if the prince of the unicorns is lost to me this year—well, perhaps you will stay with me, and we will try another spring."

Her hollow voice was sweet, soothing. Jan stumbled away from her, and she shook her head.

"Do you think to fly?" She laughed. "You cannot escape. The world's a Circle, Aljan. You will always come back to me in the end. *Come.* You know that in a moment you will come. . . ."

Then something slipped underneath Jan's heel. He felt it give like rotten fruit. A sweet stench filled his nose, and his heel felt suddenly wet and warm. He lost his footing on the slickness, falling. More shells gave under him, cutting his flank. He had stumbled amid the bed of eggs. The realization came to him as he struggled up. Gray globes crowded about his legs.

"My eggs!" the wyvern shrieked. "You fool. Come away. You will breach them!"

She writhed then, fighting toward him. Tek and Dagg held on, bracing to hold her back. Jan kicked at the eggs encircling him, tripping his limbs—he could get no footing. He plunged, trampling, but could not get free. The ground here was a shallow dish, and new eggs rolled constantly about him.

"Stop!" cried the wyrm. "You have killed my fire. Leave me my eggs."

She shook herself, furiously. Tek lost her grip and was thrown. The white wyrm staggered Dagg with a blow. He dropped her head; his legs folded. Jan hardly marked it. He stood astonished, the sick-sweet savor choking him. All about him lay fragments of egg. Broken shell ground underneath his heels. His legs were wet to hock and knee. Only one egg remained unbreached. The wyvern lunged for it. Jan sprang between her and the egg.

"Let me have it," screamed the wyrm. "What good is it to you?"

"Wyverns!" Jan thundered back at her, and it was his new voice again, resonant and strong. "I know your kind to the marrow of the bone—for you have been in my head for a long time now, uninvited guest. Did you think I would not know the things that tempt a wyvern?"

He felt the egg against his fetlock and kicked it very gently—not enough to breach it, only enough to make it roll. He kicked it again, carefully, backing toward the near wall and keeping his eye on the white wyrm the whole time; for a stratagem had come to him.

The wyvern slithered after him. Beyond her in the dimness he saw Tek getting unsteadily to her feet, Dagg shaking his head as though stunned. Jan came up against the wall behind the wyvern's nest, and held the egg between his hind heel and the stone.

 "Give it to me," the wyvern said.

"What will it buy me if I do?" Jan asked her, quietly. His limbs trembled and he was breathing hard; but despite it all, he felt strangely lightheaded—for he had her, had her in his teeth now like a pard, and that sure sense of his power made him flush. He met the wyvern's eye. "What will your last egg buy?"

The wyvern watched him, shifting uneasily. Her third head flopped weakly, whimpering. Her second head gasped, bleeding from the gills.

"Name what you would have," the wyrm queen spat. "Your freedom. Your companions' lives—your father's life. Give me the egg, and I will say nothing, will not raise the alarm till you are clear of these dens."

"I did not come here of my own will," murmured Jan. A quiet rage was filling him. The egg felt smooth and fragile beneath his heel. "You brought me here with a spell of fire. All my life you have troubled me, till the wild mare had to sing away my dreams, the good ones with the bad. . . ."

The wyvern strained, writhing. Her fingers clawed her belly scales. "You have had your vengeance, and more," she cried. "My fire, my golden god is gone. All my little prits but one. Leave me that. Only that. And go."

Jan shook his head. He could not trust her. He felt the slight give of the shell beneath his hoof. The wyvern's breath hissed, trembling. The prince's son snorted. "The word of a wyvern is as good as a lie."

"How might I pursue you or give the alarm?" the wyvern demanded. "I must hide the egg before it hatches. With only one left, I dare not risk discovery. The king must never . . . ." She broke off angrily. "Give it to me. You must. Give it to me *now*."

Jan stood three-legged, eyeing her. Behind her, Dagg had gotten to his feet. Head up, Tek glanced at him, at Jan, at the wyrm. Her hoof dug a shallow scratch on the crystalline floor. Jan motioned her back from the wyvern queen.

"You might have spared yourself," he said, "if only you had let me be. Your eggs, your fire would still be yours. I did not ask to come here."

The wyvern hissed. Behind, Tek was moving too slowly.

"Tek, Dagg, get to the entryway."

The young warrior glanced at Dagg. Still he stood, shaking his head.

"Now," barked Jan.

Tek turned to Dagg and shouldered him. They circled toward the entry. The wyrm's heads turned, watching them, her eyes blazing. Jan took his heel from the egg and moved aside. Tek and Dagg were at the door.

"The egg is yours," Jan told her, halfway to the entry now himself. "Take it and use it as you will against your king. I am a unicorn. The games of wyrms are nothing to me."

The wyvern's heads snapped back around. Her main head's eyes bored into his. Those of her second fixed on the egg. She drew breath fiercely.

"Godkiller," she muttered at him. "Hoofed monster. Murderer."

He saw her body begin to shift, the hindquarters bunching, and cavaled, nervously, aware that she was planning something but not quite sure what. Though the wall still crowded him, he was out of reach of her teeth now, even if she lunged. But he dared not take his eyes from hers. Her wounded head wailed shrilly. The others hissed and gargled.

"The stings," he heard Tek cry out suddenly. "Jan, the stings!"

The wyvern twisted her lower half. He heard the sweep of scales across the floor, glimpsed the long tail lashing. There was no retreat, no room to run—the wall was at his back. He sprang hard forward, the only way she had left to him—and the sting-barbs whipped beneath his hooves.

He closed his eyes, ducking his head. His knees and forehead collided with the wyrm. She shrieked. His brow burned in a thin arc of soreness where the firebowl had touched it. He did not realize at first that his fire-tempered horn had pierced the bone of the wyvern's breast.

The claws of the wyrm's fingers raked his cheek. Jan struggled free; he stumbled back. The white wyrm reared up, up, looming above them all like a massive white tree—and then she toppled, pitching forward. The three of them shied and scattered. And as the dead wyvern came to earth, her third head struck the last egg, pashing it.

Jan found himself standing panting by Dagg.

The two of them stared at the fallen wyrm. It lay quivering, the necks twisting and twining still while the tail thrashed madly, like a murdered snake. Jan turned away. He shuddered. He felt battered, bruised to the bone. Beside him he saw Dagg champing his teeth as though they ached.

"Are you hale?" he heard Tek asking them. Her voice was low. The chamber was very still, save for the slither of the wyrm.

"Hale enough," Jan murmured. The sweet flush of power had faded from him.

Tek snorted. There was blood on her neck and shoulders where the wyvern had cuffed her. "We heard your voice coming up from the ground, and the white wyrm baiting you," she said. "We followed it down."

"Aye," said Jan, "I know it," for he did know. He had seen it in the fire: companions searching for him, aboveground, below. Tek glanced at him keenly, surprised. He turned to Dagg then, as he realized his friend had been eyeing him as well.

"Why did you slip away?" Dagg asked. "Was it a spell she put on you?"

"Yes—no," said Jan. How to explain it? He himself scarcely understood. It had been half her spell, and half something within himself.

Dagg's eyes had grown more puzzled still. "If it wasn't," he whispered, "if it wasn't that . . . ." He glanced at Tek uncertainly, then back to Jan. "You'd only to ask me, and I'd have gone, too."

Jan felt his throat tighten suddenly. He drew breath to speak, but Tek cut him off.

"Hist, come," she said. "Another time. Let's be gone from here. The others must be halfway out of the hills by now, and who knows whether our noise may have wakened the wyrms?"

Jan felt his blood quicken then. She had given Dagg's shoulder a nip to turn him, and then sprung after him herself. Jan followed. Beside the wall the dead wyrm lay twitching, its long necks and tail knotting and unknotting.

"Mind the stings," he heard Tek murmur. "They're poison still."

Dagg gained the hall, disappearing through the natural doorway, then Tek. But just as Jan reached the threshold, he glanced back into the darkened chamber, at the white sunray and the trampled eggs, at the drowned altar and the writhing wyrm.

And he felt a prick in his left hind heel—a nettle sting, no more. And looking down, he saw the longest, middle point of the wyvern's tail just grazing his fetlock. He stared at it, uncomprehending. The white wyrm shuddered and at last was still.

Jan's legs had carried him through the doorway's arch and out into the hall before he was aware—not a half pace behind the others. He could hear them just ahead, but his gaze was fixed over one shoulder at the chamber, a hollow of darkness behind.

The stinging in his fetlock had begun to burn. Then panic surged in him, and disbelief. The wyrm was dead—how could she strike? How could a dead wrym's sting be poison still? Perhaps—perhaps Tek had been mistaken, and there was nothing to fear. But it was useless, trying to game himself. For he had begun to feel, unmistakably, the warmth of poison spreading upward from the wound.

They galloped up the curving corridor. Light wells cast wan illuminations in the gloom. The crystal resin underfoot muffled the clatter of their hooves. Jan's heel felt hot and weak, the smoke of rosehips in his blood balmy and cool. The corridor stretched on before him, and he realized they had already passed the sloping side alley down which he had come. Tek and Dagg must have found their way in by another path.

Jan found himself hard-pressed to keep abreast of Tek. Their pace made it impossible for him to limp. Hot pain crept upward into his thigh muscle. The cooling smoke in his blood seemed to mingle with the venom, easing it a little. Jan shook his head and tried desperately not to think of it. There was nothing to be done for it now.

The pathway over which they ran had leveled some. Fewer light wells illumined the gloom. Dagg's form was a paleness in the dimness ahead. The fire had reached Jan's hip joint now. Each stride was agony. All around them was stillness and the dark. The harshness of their breath, the muffled tatting of their hooves only deepened the quiet.

Jan champed his teeth, too weak now to keep up with Tek. He fell back, his nostrils straining.

His breath was coming very short. The venom burned slowly along his back toward the shoulder blades. His back legs were stumbling. Up ahead, Dagg came abruptly to a halt. Tek did the same. They moved forward cautiously then, heads lifted, nostrils wide. Jan stumbled after them.

They entered a great hall, with archways to many side chambers opening along the far walls to left and right, but few light wells pierced the high, dim ceiling. Their footfalls echoed in the vast, deserted dark. Jan felt the immense weight of earth pressing down from above, and his skin tremored and twitched. After a moment, he realized the subtle smell of rotting flowers had grown much stronger here. His eyes grew more accustomed to the gloom.

And he saw the wyverns then, vague glimpses through the dark doorways opening into the hall. They lay in heaps, dozing, sharing their warmth. Coiled into weird shapes, pale pearl in color, they barely seemed to breathe. The hall rustled with their soft sighing. Jan felt the poison in his breast dripping against his heart, working down his forelimbs, inching up his neck.

He stumbled into Tek and gasped in surprise. She shushed him. They had entered a narrow exit tunnel. The floor here rose, veering, the slope growing steep. Jan stumbled again, the sound of it loud in his own ears. Leaning against Tek, he staggered upward along the rising tunnel.

"What is it? What's wrong?"

Jan heaved himself over another shallow ripple in the floor and struggled on. He saw Dagg glancing back.

"I've been stung," Jan panted, looking at neither of them. The panic had left him, and the disbelief. He felt only despair. "The wyvern stung me on the heel."

He heard Dagg's quick drawn breath, felt Tek's teeth closing over the nape of his neck. His knees were giving way.

"Dagg, help me," he heard Tek hissing through a mouthful of his mane.

The two of them supported him between their shoulders, kept him from leaning, sinking. Jan sagged, but still he fought to gather his legs and make them obey. The poison had reached his head. His thoughts were made of water now, shifting and spangling. He could not keep his head up, gazed dully at the ground. His eyes felt glazed.

The tunnel canted upward, up, tipping crazily. More and more light poured into the passage. It hurt his eyes; he had to squint. He heard Tek and Dagg laboring to breathe, felt their sides pressing against his own. The tunnel's entrance passed overhead. He felt a sudden rush of light and air—it seemed to beat about him like wings. They were outside, and the daylight was blinding.

He felt Tek beside him shying suddenly, and felt her sharp hiss of surprise. Dagg sidled, whickering. Jan dragged his head up and peered through the blaze before him. The sky was a vault of blue flame all around. The edge of the milkwood grove twenty paces distant looked smoky and cool.

A figure stood before them at the wood's edge, looking shadow-colored against the bright glare of the sky. Very graceful and long of limb—Jan knew this unicorn. It was . . . it was . . . the poison eating up his mind had burned the name away.

The figure was coming toward him now. He wanted to go to it, but his limbs were made of shifting earth, of wind, and refused to bear his weight. He realized he was falling, slowly, and could not feel the ground beneath him, so that even as he came to rest upon his side, it felt as though he were falling still. The blood in his body danced with heat, and he gazed with one eye at the fire-white sun, floating above him on a blue lake of sky.

DREAMS

The grassy ground where he had fallen felt hard and somehow distant. Jan closed his eye to the brightness of the sun and the shadows of unicorns standing above him. Darkness and fire, then, and for a while he knew nothing but that his blood was burning and he was growing weaker, very weak, like a newborn foal.

At last he began to see again, as through a haze, and hear muffled sounds; but still, there was a distance. A red mare—Jan recognized her somehow, but could not say from where. It was she, he realized, who had stood at the wood's edge. Her coat was deep rose, the color of milkwood flowers. Her eyes, like Tek's, were green.

Jan sensed the fear and tension in her. Her shoulder blades were tight with it, her mouth gone dry. He had entered into her somehow, as in a dream, and could feel her every sensation as if it were his own. She had left the others now and was descending into the wyverns' dens, through the hall of sleepers, through the tunnels and turns. She moved deliberately, as if she knew the way.

Jan felt himself returning to his companions then. Tek was standing over something that lay near the cave's entrance, shadowing it from the sun. She was trembling—strange, for the day was warm—and her teeth were clenched. Dagg returned to her with a branch of rosebuds from the grove. He and she chewed them urgently and crushed them beneath their heels. The taste upon their tongues was pungent sweet.

The red mare rejoined them. Something huge and loose and pale shimmered as it trailed on the ground behind her. She held a fold of it in her teeth: the skin of the three-headed wyvern. Upon it lay a golden bowl. Jan felt the wyrm's blood sting the red mare's skin, her own sweat smarting in her eyes. They were dragging the skin behind them now, all three of them. It had become very heavy for some reason. They sweated and struggled. Wyrm's blood tasted bitter in their mouths.

Then he glimpsed himself upon the wyrmskin, lying beside the golden bowl, and realized it was he they bore through the milkwood grove. Even as they worked, he was aware of an image of himself in their minds, dying. That puzzled him. He had forgotten all about the wyvern's sting.

The heat of his blood rose, and he wished he could be cool again. His mind seemed to be floating still, a few paces above his own body. The eyes of the dark colt below him rolled and fluttered beneath their lids. His breath came short. His limbs twitched now and again as though he dreamed.

Jan felt his awareness lifted away then, from his body, from the milkwood grove. He glimpsed the rest of the pilgrim band at the edge of the Hallow Hills, Korr arguing once more with Teki, then with others. He watched the prince turn back toward the hills, the others going on reluctantly, to wait a little distance out on the Plain.

The grasslands fanned out before him in their vastness, and Jan felt himself skimming, as from a great height, like a bird, southward toward the Summer Sea. The unicorn valley loomed suddenly before him, and he saw his mother, heavy in foal, trotting restlessly about the verges of the birthing grove. Later, he saw the unicorns in a great Circle, wailing, "He is dead, he is dead!" and dancing the funeral dance used only for those of the prince's line.

His thoughts shifted then, altering entirely. For a moment, he became a gryphon, two gryphons, slipping into the Pan Woods under cover of cloud. Then a pan crouched two-footed among the shadows, with others of his kind. A band of *ufpútlak,* four-foots, was filing by—unicorns, by the scent of them. The pan fingered his fire-hardened stake. Trespassers. Then a banded pard sprang from the grass upon the Plain. A blue mare shied and kicked her in the ribs. Jan watched, merging into them, sometimes the mare and sometimes the pard.

Jan's blood grew hotter then, writhing hot, and

 he felt his distant body twitch and moan. Thirst

burned in him. He saw a swirl of many beasts, dust-blue herons enacting their courting rites beside the Summer Sea. He saw creatures with stiff paddles for limbs and broad, flat tails, blow-holes on their brows, and unicorns' horns growing from their mouths.

He saw the sinuous red dragons tunneling their Smoking Hills; gryphons flocked on broken mountainsides, screaming to drive out the hated unicorns. He saw the wyvern king drowsing deep in his own chamber, guarding a flickering torch and brooding subtle, seven-stranded thoughts.

But the last beasts he saw were not wyverns, nor dragons, nor gryphons, nor pards. They stood upon two legs like goatlings, but their lower limbs were straighter and less shaggy. Among them moved many unicorns, but solid-hoofed and without horns. The two-foots bound them with cords and set them to dragging great loads on wooden discs that rolled like eyes.

He caught sight of one of the hornless ones, a red roan mare, very long-limbed and clean-moving: a young beauty. Her dark mane stood upright along her neck. Her body was draped and tangled with cords. She balked, snorting. The two-foots rushed and struck at her, shouting, dragging at the cords until she reared up screaming and flailing.

The glimpse melted away. The whole world had begun to fill his eye. He merged into forests, and the wind riffled his branches. Trees rose and died; new seedlings grew. Then he was grassland, rolling and measureless. Kites wheeled above him, circling a dead Renegade.

He was sea, suddenly—green, surging, and salt—a river of ocean that girdled the world. And then he was earth, massive and still, underlying the forests, the grasslands, even the sea. He was fire, liquid stone, moving under the earth and forcing the crack. Its heat felt like his own blood, simmering.

Then he was air, a turbulent sky, heavy with clouds that blotted the sun. Great stormcells roiled toward the upper thinness, and then, blanching cold, spilled their moisture in torrents of wind-whipped rain. A band of tiny, single-horned creatures fled before him.

Jan felt himself spinning, stretching down from the clouds. He whirled, skimming the Plain, slinging up great gouts of earth and joying in the destruction. *I, too,* he heard the storm thunder. *I, too, am part of the dance.*

Storm faded, dissipated. The sky cleared. The sun sank and stars appeared. Jan felt himself among the stars, high over the earth. And the stars were moving, all things about him in the velvety blackness moving. And someone was beside him. Though he could see nothing of it, he was aware of a presence stretching away from him on all sides. It surrounded the stars, and was within the stars, and *was* the stars.

"What are you?" he heard himself asking. He was not afraid. "Who are you?"

"Your guide," the presence answered, and her

voice was so familiar to him, Jan felt unexpectedly weak with relief. But he could not say from where or when he knew her.

"Where are you?" he asked. "What are you called?"

A pause in which the whole universe seemed to wait.

"You name me." The answer came from everywhere, within him and without.

"Alma," he breathed.

"Aye," the presence answered. "Come. I will show you a thing."

At her words, he felt himself buoyed farther from the world, lifted higher among the stars. The air about him thinned and vanished, but he felt it go without distress—though were it not for the venom in his blood, he would have frozen. He gazed down and saw white mist enveloping the world.

"Tell me now," the presence said, "what do you see?"

"I see the world," Jan told her, "bright as sea-fire. It is round, a swirl of colors, turning upon itself like someone dancing."

"And?"

"And," answered Jan, "I see the pitted moon before it, ghost-lit, dancing above the world."

"And?" With a smooth, windless motion, they drew back even farther from the planet and its moon.

"I see the world and the moon," said Jan, "dancing around a pain-bright sun, with other worlds and moons of amber, mauve, and lichen-green, both larger and smaller, some nearer and some farther away."

"And now?"

They pulled back rapidly. The sun grew very small, a yellow glint among the other, whiter stars. The gulf between the pricks of light was black as nothing. The burning stars floated like firefish in the void.

"I see the sun, small as a star among other stars, some blue-white, some rosy, some red-yellow."

"Your sun *is* a star," the presence told him. "And?"

They moved back now in a headlong rush.

"I see," said Jan, softly, "the stars in a great swirl, slowly turning like some vast, spiral flower; and in the distance, I see more starflowers, some blue, some red—many of them, and all turning."

"So," the presence told him, "now you have seen more than any living creature from your world has ever seen."

Jan gazed at the fiery pinwheels arrayed around him, all leisurely spinning. He watched what seemed a long time, saying nothing, until at last he felt himself beginning to descend. The swirls of stars below grew greater, brighter, enveloping him. He struggled, uselessly.

"But," he cried out, "is there not more?"

The presence was still beside him, had never left

him. "Infinitely more, Aljan," she told him. "And you shall see it all, one day. But now our time is short."

Jan cast a long, longing glance after the bright, turning swirls, contracting to the size of stars among the other stars. They were nearing his own sun now, with its own little dance of worlds. The closeness of their passing beside the yellow star made Jan's blood sizzle. He and his guide hovered above the swirling, blue-white planet, its moon overlying it like a disc upon a disc.

"Why have you shown me this thing?" he asked.

"What have I shown you?" countered his guide.

"You . . . ." He faltered. "You have shown me the great dance, the Cycle—the one the Renegade spoke of, the one beyond even our own moon and sun. You have shown me the stars' dance."

"Aye," the presence said. "And what is my Dance?"

"It is motion," Jan told her, "energy, turning."

"It is rest and stillness also," she replied.

"Is it life, then?" Jan answered. "All things that live."

"Life, aye," the presence nodded. "And . . . ."

"And?" Jan murmured.

"The wyverns also are part of my Cycle, and murderous gryphons and wheeling kites. Fire which can destroy and the Serpent-cloud which flings all things to dust."

"Death, too," ventured Jan, "is in the Dance."

A little silence then.

"Why have you brought me here?" Jan started. "No one of my people ever has had such a vision as this."

"Ah, so you see this for a vision." The presence smiled; he felt her smile. "Well, you are a dreamer, well used to dreams."

He denied it with his thoughts. "I never dream."

The presence laughed. "Jah-lila took away the waking memory of your dreams. This day you have won them back again."

Jan shook himself. "Tell me why . . . ."

Again the presence's quiet laugh. "So importunate! But is this not what you have always wanted, to apprehend the workings of the Dance? You have looked for it only half knowing, and found it only in little bits: in the roiling of stormclouds and the workings of fire, in the fluting of pans dancing under the moon—in the depths of danger in a gryphon's eye. In the rolling vastness of grasslands that call out, 'What lies beyond me? Come see!' "

Her voice had grown so familiar now, as though she knew him to the marrow of the bone. He had not known even a god could read his inmost heart. "What are you, then?"

"I am Mystery," she told him, "that goads intelligent beings to understanding. I am Curiosity. I am Solution. I am what is, demanding to be known. Those things that you have always been asking, I have answered now, a little."

"No!" cried Jan. "You have given me only questions, a thousand more."

"Good," the presence laughed. "Spend your energies seeking their answers, not on colts' games and trickstering." Jan flinched a little beneath her bluntness. "Understand things, Aljan," his guide told him, "by learning to think as they do: enter in. Study the world and see how it works—make it work your own ends, if you can."

"But what are my ends to be?" Jan burst out.

A long silence. At last she said, "I leave that to you."

"Then why was I alone chosen to see these things?"

"Many have I given this vision to, Jan," she said. "Though none till now have I let return."

"But I will return."

He felt her nod of affirmation and fell silent then. He could think of nothing. He understood nothing.

"Come now," his guide replied, a little mocking. "You cannot be so dumbstruck as all that. Have I not whispered all your life that you were born to see great things?"

Jan felt his mind constrict. "Great things," he murmured. "Will I . . . will I see the coming of the Firebringer?"

"You have already," his guide returned. "The Firebringer is among you now."

"Is it . . . ?" Jan stumbled to a stop. He hardly dared say it. "Will my father be the one?"

The presence seemed to turn away a little then. "Perhaps," she said, indifferently. "Who knows?"

"You do!" cried Jan.

The goddess laughed. "Aye. I do that. But that is not yet yours to know."

"My people need a Firebringer," Jan insisted. "To rout the wyrms. The Vale is growing too close for us, and the gryphon said . . . ."

"I know what the gryphon said."

A sudden urgency burned in Jan. "Her people hate us. They are planning to fly against us and drive us from the Vale. . . ."

"Have you told your father that?" the presence interrupted.

Jan shook his head, startled. The gryphon had charmed him—he realized that now—telling him while he gazed into her eye as in a dream. He had not remembered until this moment.

The goddess said, "But if you won back the Hallow Hills before that time, the gryphons could have your Vale and welcome; there would be no need to war." It was as if she had spoken his own thoughts back at him. "Is that what you were beginning to say?"

"My father is a great warrior," Jan answered her. "He could rout the wyverns from the Hallow Hills. But the legend says he must have fire. The wyverns' dens would go up in a blaze if . . . ."

"There are many kinds of fire, Aljan."

Jan hardly heard. "But my father knows nothing at all of fire. I am the only unicorn who knows—but I know nothing, hardly anything!"

"Then you'd best make a study of it, hadn't you?" the presence remarked. "You've only a few years' time before the gryphons fly. List, now," his guide said suddenly. "The time grows very short. Ask me what question you will, and I will answer."

"I . . ." started Jan. He could feel the vision's end looming, and burst out with the first question that came to him. "Why do the gryphons hate us?"

"You already know the beginning of that."

"Why do the pans speak so differently from us, then?" He struggled. Time slipped from him. His body burned.

"Again," the goddess told him, "you may find that for yourself. Hist, be quick."

"Then, then . . ." stammered Jan. He racked his thoughts for some riddle worthy of a god. "Why must we bind ourselves to the Circle of Warriors?"

"Who tells you you must? Not I. I do not make kings, or Rings of Law. Those things are yours to make, or to unmake, just as you choose."

"Why does my mother tell me to follow my own heart, not Korr's?"

"Ask her," the goddess said.

"Who is the Red Mare the Renegades spoke of?"

"Ask her."

Jan felt himself beginning to fall. He struggled desperately to remain aloft. "But why does your voice sound so familiar to me? I have never met you before in dreams."

"Whom do I sound like?" the presence demanded, bearing him up for a moment more.

"Like Jah-lila," said Jan, "and like Korr. Like

Ses my dam and like Khraa the king. Like Tek and Dagg—Tas, Teki, Leerah . . . ."

"Who else?"

"Like the three-headed wyvern," Jan replied. "Like the gryphon in the cave, like the fluting of pans, or Renegades crying, like . . . ."

"Like?"

"Like sea, like earth shifting, like wind and like fire."

"And?"

"Like myself," said Jan, coming suddenly breathless to a halt. He had quit struggling. "Like me."

"I *am* you," the Mother-of-all replied, "and much, much more besides. I am everything you have ever known and that has ever been. I surround you all, and am within you, and am you. You are my kindling; I am the Fire. I am the Circle. I am the Dance. Learn to know me. Come." A moment passed. "The time's at hand. You must return."

Then he felt what had been supporting him vanish. He was descending in a rush toward the bright, pale-blue world and the gray pitted moon before it. The world grew large, more varicolored. Its gray companion, within its disc, also increased. Jan felt himself falling toward the heart of the moon.

"Alma," he cried out. There was no need. The presence had not left him. "Did you not tell me I would return to the world?"

The other nodded in his mind. "Aye. Back to the Hallow Hills and your three companions."

The moon loomed, burning silver in the white light of the sun. Perfectly round, it seemed to lie upon the surface of the world like a lake of still, bright water.

"But Alma," cried Jan, "the moon . . . ."

"Nay, Jan," the goddess told him, departing now. "The Mirror of the Moon."

He felt a splash and heard the sound of it. Then he was aware of three unicorns: Tek, the red mare, and Dagg. They had staggered from the woods, dragging the wyvern skin. Stumbling under its weight in the midafternoon sun, they waded out into the water.

He felt the wet slosh about their knees, and the strain against their teeth and jaws. The wyrmskin on which he lay touched the surface and buoyed up. Cool liquid spilled in at the slack places, bathing him. The fire in his blood swabbed out.

He heard the angry hiss of water mingling with the wyrm's blood on the skin, and the air was suddenly thick with acrid steam. He heard whinnies of alarm, then snorts and choking. The wyvern skin fell abruptly slack. It floated. The golden bowl slid off and sank.

He could not get his eyes open, could not see what was happening. He struggled weakly to raise his head. There was thrashing in the water nearby him: he heard gasps, and then two, three dull thuds upon the sand. The acrid air around him hung suddenly, utterly silent, until the harsh vapor invaded his senses at last. He knew nothing more.

Jan came again into awareness slowly. He felt himself floating, the coolness of water against one side, and the soft, sinuous membrane bearing him up. The sun on his other side was warm and drying. He opened his eyes and blinked. Raising his head with difficulty against the yielding surface of the skin, he saw he lay on the sacred pool, near shore. The sun overhead shone midafternoon.

He floundered off the floating hide and onto the white sand of the shallow bottom. His limbs no longer burned with fire. The golden bowl lay submerged, sun-gleaming, a half pace from him. He got to his feet and champed his teeth. His nose and heel were plastered with chewed milkwood buds. The taste of water in his mouth was sweet. He bent and took a long drink from the pool.

Lifting his head, he spotted the others. They lay on the bank, fallen in midstride. Jan felt his heart go cold a moment, but then he saw the rising and falling of their sides: they were alive. He waded toward them, and halted in the shallows beside the red mare.

He recognized her now. She was Jah-lila, Tek's mother, the lone unicorn—she his father had called once, long ago, to come sing away his dreams. Jan bent and nudged her with his nose. She stirred then, snorting, and rolled to get her legs under her, but did not rise.

"Well glad I am to see you alive, prince-son," she told him at last, then shook her head, as if groggy still. She managed a laugh. "The Mirror of the Moon is strong proof against poison."

Her voice was very like Tek's, but fuller and a little more deep. Jan nodded, eyeing her, feeling strange and unsurprised.

"I heard you singing on the night of Moondance," was all he could think of to say.

The wild mare nodded. "Aye. I was singing a charm on you, little prince, to keep you from seeing me. But my power over you is all ashes now." She sighed, still smiling, and gazed away. "No ears but yours were meant to hear that song, but I think Tek heard it, too, for she came looking for me." Jah-lila glanced at him.

"She looked for you in the Pan Woods, too," said Jan, "and again upon the Plain. But she never . . ."

The other laughed, gently. All her moves were careful and unhurried. "I did not mean for her to find me—or for you. But of course it was mostly your father I meant to . . ." But Jan hardly heard.

"You called out to me in the Pan Woods," he

said suddenly, "and led us away from the others to the goatling's Ring." The realization jarred him. "You began to bury the Renegade."

The red mare nodded. "I did those things."

Jan bit his breath, stopping himself. "The Serpent-cloud," he said. "You led the storm away."

The healer's mate smiled. "So you saw me then, too?" She sighed, laughing. "Already you were stealing back your dreams."

A little silence then.

"Why did you come?" he asked, at last.

"On account of you," Tek's mother said, studying him now. The green in her eyes was very dark. "I meant to stand unseen among the milkwood at Vigil and sing back to you what I had taken once, at your father's bidding—for none may behold his fate upon the Mirror who cannot dream."

She shook her head.

"I told your father that, when first I sang you, that you must have back your dreaming sight before you got your beard. But he did not wish it, argued against it. He is very much afraid of dreams, ever since, a very long time past, a wyvern tried to speak to him in one."

Jan felt his skin prickling.

The red mare said, "He did not send word to me, as I had bidden him, when you were to go on Pilgrimage. Your mother did that."

Jan gazed at nothing, striving desperately to remember what the wyvern had said: *I tried to reach your father once . . . when Korr was young and not yet prince . . . tried to send him a dream to ruin him, send him running wild Renegade across the Plain. . . .* The red mare gazed back at Jan, her quiet tone gone rueful now.

"But I could not be with you on this night just past. I had to run a long way across the Plain with that storm in my teeth before it blew itself to nothing. It has taken me all this time returning."

Jan shook his head. His mind was full. He could not take in any more. "You could have given me back my dreams in the Vale, at Moondance."

Lying with folded legs beside the water there, I shook my head. "No. I took your dreams by the dark of the moon, and so by the dark must they return."

Would he understand that? I hoped so. The ways of magic are limited, and strange. Then I told him a little more of the truth, speaking slowly, that he might follow me.

"But there is another reason I held back. On a night many years past before ever you were born, prince-son, when first I felt the weight of a horn upon my brow and my body becoming a unicorn's, I stood beside this Mere, beholding a dream. It told me I must one day return to the Hallow Hills, and deliver a unicorn safe out of a wyvern's belly."

I stood up then, shaking the sand and damp from me, unsure how much of what I had said he had been able to grasp. The young prince continued to stare at me, and for the first time he seemed to realize how my black mane stood up in a brush along my neck and that my tail fell full and silky as a mane. No beard grew silken on my chin, no feathery fringe about my heels. He saw my hooves then, which are round and single as the day I was foaled, for all that a horn now sprouts on my brow.

For I was not born among the unicorns. In that, the Renegades were right. I come from a place far to the western south, beyond the shallows of the Summer Sea. But I fled away in time, and found the unicorns in their Vale. Their beauty, when first I saw them, was so great I ached to join them. But I held back, sick with longing, for I was not like them—until I learned of a sacred well across the Plain that makes the unicorns what they are, and a young prince told me the way.

But that is another tale.

"What are you?" whispered the prince's son, falling back a pace to gaze on my beardless chin and single hooves.

I tossed my head. What could I tell him? He wanted it all in a word, and I myself only barely understood what it was I had been, and was now, and was yet becoming. Still, I tried to answer him.

"I am the midwife," I told him, "who stands between the womb of Alma and the world. I do not make, but I help what has been made to be born."

Did that make sense to him? I studied his face, but what he made of my words I could not tell. I tried again.

"I am a dreamer, and a little of a magicker. There

is a race of two-footed creatures, Aljan, great movers and builders. They keep many burden-beasts to haul and carry for them." I could not quite keep the bitterness out of my voice as I said the last. "I was such a bearer once, until I came away."

Then the young prince surprised me. "I saw you," he told me, soft, and did not draw away from me, as others do. "I saw you among the two-foots in my vision." And I knew then, for him to have seen that, he must be a far-dreaming seer indeed. He looked at me. "But your coat was another color, then. It was roan."

I smiled a little. "The blossoms of the milkwood which I ate made my coat this color, and the bitter waters of the Mere gave me a horn."

"So you are the Red Mare the Renegades spoke of," Jan answered quietly. "They said my father helped you somehow."

I nodded, remembering. "He was very like you then—wild, hotheaded, and proud, though not so clever or far-seeing by half. Though it was against all custom, he told me the way to the unicorn's Mere and, in doing so, broke the Ring of Law and opened himself to a wyvern's spells. I kept them at bay, barely."

The young prince stood, not seeing me, looking inward then. I told him, "And afterward, I sang much of that memory out of your father's mind, just as I once sang away your dreams. One day perhaps I will give it back to him—if he will have it back. He is not a seer, Jan, and has no understanding of magic and dreams."

The other's dark eyes pierced me then, urgent and fire bright. "Give me the tale," he whispered. "I must know. Sing me the tale."

"I *will* give you the tale," I replied, turning away. "But not just now. Another time."

The prince's son said nothing then, watching me.

"Are you not cold, little prince, with your coat still full of water?" I asked him. Behind me I could hear Tek beginning to stir. "Shake off," I said, turning to rouse her. "The afternoon grows late."

Jan shook himself. He *was* cold. The water from his coat showered onto Dagg, who stirred and at last got groggily to his feet. I roused my daughter. She stood up, draggled and chilled, and shook herself. Jan came near us, and though from time to time I caught his eyes darting guardedly at me, full of questions—a thousand questions—he seemed willing to curb them, for now.

"Drink," he told us, bending again to the pool himself. "The water's sweet."

"Sweet?" I heard my daughter say as she waded out into the Mere. "I tasted it this dawn. It's bitter salt."

Jan shook his head, gazing at her again as he had gazed at her for the first time in the milkwood grove, with new eyes. "Sweet now. Taste it."

When first I had sipped of the Moon's Mere, years ago, it made me ill. Then I could stomach no more than a half-dozen swallows before I began to shiver and sweat, and stagger a little in my walking, so strange had been the taste, so mineral.

But now as I bent my head with the others to drink, the water was cool and without taint. It washed the bitter taste of the wyrm's blood from my mouth.

Jan felt his strength beginning to return. He no longer felt hollow, famished, though he had not eaten in more than a day. The water alone seemed to satisfy him. The rosebuds plastered to his nose and heel had long since sluiced away. His fetlock still felt sore from the wvyern's sting, his brow tender from the firebowl's burning. But even those aches were beginning to fade. His forelock fell thickly into his eyes.

"It is," Dagg was saying, raising his mouth from the water. "It is sweet."

I heard a little noise behind us suddenly and turned, glimpsed something drawing near through the milkwood trees. Then the prince of the unicorns emerged from the grove. I and two of the others started. I had not been expecting him. Only Jan seemed unsurprised.

His father stood a moment, open-mouthed, and stared at us, seeming almost more astonished to see me than he was to see his son. But it was Jan and the others he spoke to in the end, ignoring me as though I were some haunt or dream.

"What game is this?" he snorted, stamping his hooves as he always did whenever he was baffled or made uneasy. "Where have you been, the three of you? Traipsing these groves at some colts' play while your elders and companions ran themselves to rags hunting you."

He was all terrible thunder and princely affront. I started to speak, but the princeling stepped past me. He would need no mediator ever again. Approaching, he stood before his father without flinching and said, "No games. Tek, Dagg, and I have been killing *that,* lest she rouse the wyrms to fall upon us all."

He nodded toward the wyvern skin, which lay still floating on the pool. My daughter and Dagg dragged it from the water and spread it out upon the sand. The prince fell silent then, staring at it. Jan turned away, and I stood off with Korr a few moments, telling him from my daughter's account what had befallen his son in the wyvern's den.

The young prince and his two companions meanwhile had raised the skin and shaken off the sand. They let the wind lift it streaming into the air and laid it upon the low branches of the near milkwood trees. Like a great pennant, a banner, it blazed and shimmered in the hot spring sun.

I left off with Korr, and he said no more to Jan, either in praise or in rebuke. I think it puzzled him to have suddenly a son who neither trembled at his frown nor needed his approval to feel proud. Instead the prince of the unicorns gauged the sun.

"Come," he said at last. "We must be off. The hour is late, and the others wait for us upon the Plain."

"I'll leave you then," I said, shaking the silence from me.

Korr stared at me. "You'll not run the journey home with us?" he began.

I shook my head. "Someone must go before you, and sing the tale." I gave him no time to argue with me. "Farewell, my prince, my brave daughter, Dagg."

And oh, the look Tek gave me then, as if to say, "Off again? Off again, Mother, and only just met." Would she ever guess why I had left her to be raised in the Vale by the one who calls himself my mate, or ever trust that there are reasons for everything I do? I glanced from her to Jan—then shook such thoughts from me. I could not stay.

To the young prince, I said, "I'll leave you with your father now, prince-son, but one day, in a year or two year's time, you must come away with me. I'll teach you things a prince should know."

He barely understood me. I did not mean him to. That day was yet a long way off. Then, giving to none of them time to stay me or make reply, I tossed my head and wheeled away, galloping off through the flowering milkwood trees, until their boles and the distance hid me from their view.

Nothing of note befell them in the Hills after I left them. I have never asked the prince's son how much he told his father of his game of wits with the wyvern queen or of his vision in the womb of Alma—little, I think. Nor have I troubled to discover how they spent their half month returning over the Plain, save only that it was a good running and swift, without mishap.

I reached the Vale two days before them, and told the whole herd assembled how the prince's son had saved the pilgrim band from wyvern's jaws by battling their queen to the death below ground. The old king Khraa was much impressed, fairly burst with pride, calling his grandson a worthy heir.

But I noticed the gray king looked older than when I had seen him last, barely a month ago. He moved with a stiffness in his bones. Alma was calling him. He and I both knew it, and nothing lay within my power either to stem that call or stay his answering.

When the prince-son, his father, and the others returned home, two hours before sunset on the day of the full moon, that night each month which the unicorns of the Vale call Moondance, I was already a half day gone. Many of the mares the pilgrims had left in foal the month before now had new foals or fillies at their sides, Jan's mother among them. And the king was dead.

☆

So when the prince led his pilgrims home at last, he found, not a gathering of welcome, but one of mourning. Dagg's father, Tas, took Korr apart to tell him of the gray king's death. They had buried him the day before, unable to wait upon his son's return, for the wheel of the world must turn, and time with it.

Hearing of his father's death, Korr bowed his head and did not speak. Then he went off to the burial cliffs with a small circle of the highest elders to be made king before sunset, for the herd had been nearly two days without a king and were uneasy for want of one.

Jan stood amid the milling crowd, feeling lost and uncertain. Friends greeted the new-made warriors with joyous shouts and jostling. Others stood off quietly, recounting the death of the king. But in all the crush of kith and strangers, Jan caught no glimpse of his own dam, Ses. As he stood scanning for her, Dagg's mother came up beside him.

"You mother bade me tell you she would wait for you at the wood's edge, there."

Leerah tossed her head. Jan gave her a nod of thanks, then sprang away across the valley floor. He mounted the slope, passing his own cave, and headed toward the line of trees. He saw his mother then, waiting at the wood's edge among the long, dusky shadows. Her form was the color of beeswax, of flame. A filly not more than two weeks old stood pressed to her flank.

"What will you call her?" Jan found himself saying. He had come to a halt. The filly started at the sound of his voice, pressing closer to the pale mare's side. His mother smiled.

"Lell," she answered. "We'll call her Lell."

Jan came closer. Dark amber, the filly watched him. Her brushlike, newborn's mane was blonde. Her brow bore but the promise of a horn, a tiny bump beneath the skin.

"Well met," he heard his mother saying, "my bearded boy. You'll have fine silk upon your chin by summer's end."

Jan felt a rush of pride. Already, he knew, the feathery hairs were sprouting along his jaw.

His mother said, "How was your pilgrimming?"

He shrugged, suddenly shy. "You have heard it all already from Jah-lila." She nodded and laughed. He said nothing, looking off. "I had a dream," he said at last, "upon the Mirror of the Moon. I dreamed the unicorns in mourning, crying, 'He is dead. He of the line of Halla, dead!' " He looked at Ses. "I thought they wept for me."

His mother laughed again, but very softly now. "I knew you would return to me. Korr feared you would fly off breakneck at the first opportunity—run wild Renegade across the Plain. But I did not."

Jan frowned. "Why would he think that? My place is here, among the Circle." Already he had forgotten ever dreaming himself outcast.

Ses nodded, murmuring, "You are prince now of the Ring."

Jan gave a little start, then sighed. He had forgotten that. "Mother, I have seen other Rings than ours. I have seen gryphons that were brave and loyal after their own kind of honor, pans dancing to reed voices under the moon, and Renegades who were not hornless, solid-hoofed or godless things."

"Aye," she told him. "That is an old mare's tale, about the Renegades."

"And I have seen a Cycle that is wider than all our smaller Rings," said Jan, "and includes them, and surpasses them. A place waits for me in that wider Ring, too. I have seen it, and cannot wake or sleep dreamless of it ever again."

He saw a slow smile light his mother's eye. "Then I am glad," she said. "All that ever I have wished is to see you follow your own heart, and no other."

She came forward and stood against him, laying her neck about his neck. Jan saw his sister, Lell, begin to suckle, butting his mother's side. He leaned against his dam, watching. After a time, he felt her warm, dry tongue stroking his shoulder. He drew back.

"What are you doing?" he began.

"Getting the dust off you," she replied. "Truth, how did you get so much into your coat? You look as though you've rolled in it."

Jan stood off and shook himself. He *had* rolled in dust. His winter coat had shed upon the Plain, coming off all in an evening in thick mats of hair. And the color beneath had been darker than the old, not a trace of sable to it. For he was black as his father beneath the shed. The color at last ran true.

But he had felt strange in his sleek new coat, like a trickster, somehow—like a thief. So he had rolled in dust to hide the color from others' eyes a few days longer. But there could be no more hiding now. He was home. He shook himself again. Dust rose like smoke from the glossy blackness of him, and hung in the still, sunlit air between the shadows.

His mother gave no indication of surprise. "And

what is that upon your brow?"

He realized then he had shaken his forelock back as well. He had not meant to. He had been letting it fall thickly into his eyes this last half month. But there could be no taking that back, either. He went to stand before his dam.

She studied the new hairs, pale as hoarfrost, growing in a thin crescent where the rim of the firebowl had burned him. He had seen them for the first time only that morning, in a pool in the Pan Woods. But he had felt them these last dozen days, growing.

"Show me the heel where the wyvern stung you."

Jan lifted his hoof and held it crooked that she might see the fetlock better. Since they had left the Hallow Hills, he had kept the spot daubed with mud on the healer's advice; but they had waded streams in the Pan Woods that day, and he had forgotten to replace the mud. The new hair covering the little spot was pale as well.

"I am the Firebringer," he said. He had not realized it until they were long out of the Hallow Hills, halfway home across the Plain. He had said nothing to anyone, till now. "I . . . I always thought it would be Korr."

Ses laughed then. "My son, I love your father well, but he is no seer of dreams."

Jan gazed at her. He could not fathom her unsurprise. Again she laughed.

"On the night of my initiation, long ago, I saw myself give birth to a flit of flame. And I have never doubted for a day what that must mean."

Then Jan said nothing for a while, for he could think of nothing. His sister Lell left off her suckling, and crept around her mother's side to look at him.

"Look," he heard Ses saying. "I see Korr across the Vale, coming back with the elders from the kingmaking." She looked at him a moment, and then off. "The sun's almost set. We should go down."

She started forward, out of the trees' shadows. He did not follow. She halted, glancing back at him.

"Do you come?"

He shook his head. "You go," he told her. "In a while."

He watched his mother descend toward the valley floor, Lell stumbling after her on long, still-awkward legs. They joined the crowd and made for the rise at the center, which Korr was now mounting. His shoulders were daubed with the red and yellow mud of the grave cliffs, that marks the new-made kings among the unicorns. Jan turned and headed upslope through the trees.

He made his way to the lookout knoll and stood only paces from the wood's edge there, from the treeless swatch where he and Tek had fought the gryphon more than a month past—it seemed a very long time ago. Jan gazed down at the milling unicorns, deep blues and scarlets mostly, a smattering of ambers, here and there a gold, a gray.

"There you are," panted Dagg, coming up the slope. "I've been looking—everyone has."

Jan nodded, not turning. He scrubbed himself absently against the rough bark of a fir. His new coat itched.

Dagg snorted and shouldered against him. "What are you doing up here?"

"It's a good spot," Jan answered. "I can watch the dance from here."

"Watch it?" cried Dagg. "You're always *watching* things. You never enter in."

"I do," said Jan. "I'm a better dancer than you."

"You are not."

They fell on each other, nipping and shoulder-wrestling. They snorted, panting—and broke off abruptly at the sound of a low, nickering laugh. Jan turned to see Tek watching from the trees.

"How did you find us?" demanded Dagg.

Tek shrugged, emerging from the trees. She turned to gaze toward the unicorns below. "I have long known all your haunts and hollows. They were mine but two years gone."

Jan and Dagg came to stand beside her. The dusk deepened. None of them spoke. The evening sky grew red.

"We should go," Dagg said.

Jan caught him back. "Not yet."

The sky above was hinting into violet. Tek turned to Jan. "They want to make you prince before the dance," she said. "It was why I came."

Jan looked at her. "Will it matter to you, when I am prince?"

He heard Dagg's laugh. His friend shouldered against him. "I never cared when you were princeling, did I?"

Tek shrugged, eyeing him with half a smile. "Princes put no fear in me."

Jan almost laughed, then caught himself. The mark of Alma rode heavy on his brow. "But what if I were more?" he said. "More than prince—would it matter?"

Dagg looked at him. "Korr's not dead yet," he said.

Then Jan did laugh. He caught Tek studying him.

"What are you talking about, little prince?" she said quietly. "Tell us."

The prince of the unicorns looked down, away. His white heel pricked him in the dark. He picked at the fir needles underfoot with that hind, cloven hoof. "Tomorrow."

Above them, the sky shaded from wine to indigo, lying smooth and cloudless as still, clear water. Night settled. A line of silver peered over the slope across the valley from them, and the dark blue of the sky grew suddenly smoky and more light. The few stars pricking the canopy above paled. Jan watched the rim of brightness edging over the hills.

"Moon's up," he heard Dagg saying. "They'll be starting the dance."

Jan drew his breath. "Full moon tonight," he murmured. "I'd forgot."

The herd below had begun to turn, slowly, a

rough, wide Ring drifting now deasil, now widdershins about the rise in the valley floor where the new king stood. Tek wheeled on Jan suddenly, gave him a smart nip on the shoulder, then bolted from beside him, tearing down the slope. Her light taunt drifted back:

"First down shall have the center of the dance!"

Jan sprang after, and heard Dagg barely a half-pace behind. They galloped breakneck, shouldering and kicking, as they raced to overtake her before she reached the bottom of the slope.

FULL CIRCLE

So it was not Jan, but I that night who watched the dancing from above. Though the others thought me gone, I had kept myself hidden on the far wooded slope where I had stood the month before. Thus I saw the pilgrims safely home, and the making of Korr into the king.

The Circle on the valley floor below me grew gradually thinner, its members fanning outward to form a greater, more circular Ring. The young prince, my daughter, and their shoulder-friend rejoined the dance now moving deasil, steadily deasil, beneath the circling moon.

I departed, and left them to their dancing. And I have come among you these many years after, you who dwell upon the Plain and call yourselves the Free People, you who know so little of your southern cousins, the unicorns of the Vale.

I have told you this tale to remind you of them, for though you have forgotten it, all unicorns were once a single tribe, just as—though you may doubt it—my people, who dwell beyond the Summer Sea, were once like yours. But this tale marks only the first night of my telling. Come to me tomorrow evening, and I will tell you the rest.